ROBERT SWINDELLS
STAYING UP

CORGI BOOKS

STAYING UP
A CORGI BOOK: 0 552 545864

First published in Great Britain by Oxford University Press

PRINTING HISTORY
Oxford University Press edition published 1986
Corgi Freeway edition published 1990
Corgi edition reissued 1998

Set in 12/13pt Palatino
by Phoenix Typesetting, Ilkley, West Yorkshire.

Corgi Books are published by Transworld Publishers Ltd,
61–63 Uxbridge Road, Ealing, London W5 5SA,
in Australia by Transworld Publishers (Australia) Pty. Ltd,
15–25 Helles Avenue, Moorebank, NSW 2170,
and in New Zealand by Transworld Publishers (NZ) Ltd,
3 William Pickering Drive, Albany, Auckland.

Made and printed in Great Britain by
Cox and Wyman Ltd, Reading, Berkshire.

For Linda Ann Swindells

PART ONE

SING WHEN YOU'RE WINNING

The Town

You don't walk through Thorne Edge by yourself after dark. Not unless you're wrong in your head you don't. It's one of those great, sprawling estates they shoved up in the fifties to solve the housing shortage. They shoved it up so fast on the hillside north of Barfax they forgot about shops and pubs and cinemas, so if you live on Thorne Edge you have to go down town to find something to do. The sense of isolation this causes, together with the general squalor of the place, has turned some Thorne Edge residents mean. Even coppers only go in twos.

It's a funny place, Barfax. When they were building Thorne Edge it was a wool town: hulking great mills and thousands of little black houses crammed together in the valley, smoking like hell. Mucky Barfax they called it, and it was. There were people in Barfax who'd never had a lungful of clean air in their lives. You'd see them in the early mornings, coughing and hawking at bus stops.

Mucky Barfax. Where there's muck, there's brass, they used to say. There was too. People used to come from all over to work in the mills of Barfax. So many came that the town started to spread up the surrounding hillsides. Estates sprang up: red brick semis and concrete roads and patches of raw yellow clay they called gardens. Thorne Edge was one of them.

It's not like that now in Barfax. The mills have shut and they've knocked a lot of them down. A lot of the people have gone away and most of the others live out in the estates. Where the houses were there's supermarkets and warehouses and little glass office blocks, most of them empty. There's just the lamp factory now. Ambler's, where they make light bulbs and fluorescent tubes and stuff. That's where most people work. There's a big new hotel and a shopping centre and that's about it. A few pubs. They've turned some of the pubs into wine-bars.

And then there's the football ground. Hillside, home of Barfax Town. They're a Second Division side. At least, they're in the Second Division at the moment. A lot of the older fans reckon they're a Third Division side that just happened to have a good season a couple of years ago when everybody else had a bad one. They'll go back down, they keep saying. Next season, they'll go back down. They act cynical but they're proud really. Just when everything else was getting worse, Town went up. It's about the only thing Barfax has to shout about nowadays, and everybody needs something to shout about. Otherwise, what's the point?

1

Debbie giggled and twisted herself away from him. 'Geroff, Brian!' They were sitting on the wall by the Chinese chippy. It was dusk.

'What the heck's up with you? I was only—'

'I know, and in broad daylight and all. Don't you ever think of owt else, Brian Gower?'

'It's getting dark. And anyway no-one's bothered.'

'I am. And my dad would be and all if he happened to come past. He'd knock you right off this wall and drag me home by the hair. You know what he's like.'

'Yeah.' He stared at his hands, clamped in the vice of his knees, then looked sideways at her. 'How about the match tomorrow then?'

'What about it?'

'You coming?'

'Am I hummer. You know I can't stand football.'

'I came to that flippin' wolves film with you, didn't I – and I can't stand fairy-tales.'

'Don't give me that. You didn't go for the film anyway.'

'What d'you mean?'

'You know. Anyway I'm not standing on the Kop with Barry Weatherall and Aziz Khan and all them hooligans. You must think I'm daft.'

'We don't stand with them. They're the Ointment. They wouldn't have us. It'll just be me, Colin, Lee, Jeannette, and Jonathan. Jeannette comes, so I don't see why you can't.'

'Ha! That slag.'

'She's not a slag, just 'cause she supports the Town. She's a nice lass.'

Debbie pulled a face. 'Not my type. Anyway I've got to go now.' She picked up the trays with their green smears of curry sauce, put one inside the other and dropped the plastic forks in the top one. She stood up. 'I might see you in the Arndale in the morning. About ten.'

'Hang on, love.' He reached out and hooked a finger in the band of her jeans.

'What?'

'Listen. I want to ask you summat.'

'What?'

'Sit down a minute.'

She sighed and sat down with the trays on one knee. 'What?'

Brian sat forward, gazing at the pavement between his feet. He spoke without looking at her. 'It's been good, these holidays. You and me I mean. D'you want to go on?'

'What d'you mean, go on?'

'Well – it's school Tuesday. Shall we still go

12

round together, nights and weekends. Or has this been just a holiday thing?'

Debbie frowned. 'I don't know. I mean – I like you and all that. We can go on if you like, only I'm not off to football. OK?'

'Yeah.' He looked sideways at her again and grinned. 'Yeah – sure it's OK. Great. Come on then – I'll walk you home.'

'It's out of your way.'

'I'm not bothered. Anyway there's a murderer about.'

He reached for her hand but she snatched it away and held out the trays. 'Here – find a bin for these first.'

'Bin? I'm not looking for any bin. Give 'em here.' He took them from her and drop-kicked them over the wall.

'Litter-lout.'

'I know.' One of the forks had fallen by his foot. He stamped it to splinters and they walked on laughing, hand in hand.

2

Brian is a Barfax Town supporter. He lives in Willoughby Road with his mum and dad and two brothers. His sister Carole lives there too, with her baby.

Seven people in three bedrooms.

There used to be Brian's other sister, Sharon, but she got married and moved out. Brian was glad. The space she left didn't amount to much when shared among six, but they enjoyed the feel of it while it lasted.

Then Carole had the baby and they were seven again.

Carole's not married. Everybody says it doesn't matter these days but it matters to Carole. She feels guilty. She feeds her baby and he gains weight, filling Sharon's space. Carole imagines she can feel the others moving over, making room. She senses the resentment. Carole walks her baby in the night, up and down the room, shushing him in case his crying should add to his unpopularity and her own. She is nineteen and feels tired all the time.

Brian lies in his bunk. He can hear his sister's footfalls through the wall. Half a metre above him lies Mick, and just over a metre to his left Dale snores like a pig in his narrow bed.

Brian is fifteen. He thinks that someday he'll have a room of his own and he might, if he's still around. He expects to be, but that's because he doesn't know what's coming to him. Nobody does, and it's best they shouldn't. Life can play some mucky tricks on folk.

3

His dad sat hunched over the table, assembling a model aeroplane. He looked up as Brian came into the room.

'What time d'you call this, Brian?'

Brian looked at his watch. It was ten past ten. He felt like saying 'I call it five in the morning, Dad,' but he daren't. There was enough fratching these days without that. 'It's about ten, isn't it?' he said. He had dawdled home, hoping Dale and his dad might be out and Carole in bed. Mick worked in a fried chicken place and wouldn't be in till midnight. Carole wasn't there, but Dale was watching TV with his mother. They were probably skint as usual.

'It's ten past, and I said ten o'clock sharp. Where've you been?'

'He's been bothering with that lass he knocks about with,' said Dale, without taking his eyes off the screen. Dale had moped ever since the army turned him down.

'Well – I walked her home, that's all.'

'All?' His dad's eyebrows went up. 'When I was fifteen I'd never spoken to a lass, let alone seen one home, and I had to be in bed by half-past eight, and all. Lads had hobbies then – collecting and that. They'd no time for lasses.'

'Some haven't altered much neither,' said his wife drily.

'Watch your programme, you,' he growled.

'It isn't school tomorrow,' said Brian. 'And anyway, it'd be no use going to bed at half eight in this house. Too much row. I can't even get my homework done unless I go down the library.'

'I always used to manage,' his dad told him. 'And there were ten of us in a back-to-back.'

'Back-to-back?' growled Brian. 'Luxury. We lived in an old shoebox in t'gutter and there was a hundred and fourteen of us. We used to walk twenty-eight miles to t'mill every morning and when we got there we got a good hiding for breakfast – if we were lucky.'

His dad regarded him through narrowed eyes. 'Are you taking the mickey out of me, or what?'

Brian grinned. 'Not really, no. It's part of the Yorkshiremen sketch from *The Secret Policeman's Ball.* Colin's got it on video.'

'Aye well – give over being clever and get to bed. And do it quietly and all – our Carole's just got Nick off and I don't want him roaring all night again.'

Nick was eighteen months old, and teething. Brian knew Carole tried her best to keep him quiet, but he couldn't help wishing she'd hurry up and find a place of her own.

'All right then – g'night.'

Nobody answered. His dad turned the little warplane under the table-lamp, looking at it with one eye closed. Dale crushed out his rollup and started to make another. From above came the fretful whimper of a child in pain. Brian sighed and left the room, wishing he lived in a posh flat with Debbie.

4

Debbie flung herself down on the bed, reached for her radio and tuned in to The Pulse. Not too loud or it'll start them off again. Her parents had seen Brian through the curtains so she couldn't pretend she'd been out with the girls. They'd started in on her as soon as she walked through the door.

'Where've you been till this time?'

'Down town.'

'Yes, but where?'

'Giggles.'

'That's a public house, isn't it?'

'It's a wine-bar, Mum.' Her mum always said public house – never pub.

'Wine-bar or public house, it makes no difference, Deborah. You're only fourteen and you shouldn't go into drinking dens.'

'It's not a drinking den. Not when we go. They have Young Teens Night. You can only get Coke and stuff till nine o'clock, then you have to leave if you're not eighteen.'

'Nine o'clock?' Now it was Dad's turn. He

17

made a big thing out of looking at his watch. 'It's five to ten now. If you left this Giggles place at nine where've you been since?'

Debbie sighed. 'It's a twenty-minute walk up from town, Dad. We called at the Chinese chippy, then Brian walked me home. That's all.'

'Yes,' her father pursued, 'and that's another thing, young lady. I thought I told you to drop this Brian character. Your mother and I know a bit about his background and we don't care for him.'

'Background?' cried Debbie. 'What sort of a word's that? What's wrong with his background, as you call it?'

'Well, in the first place he lives on Thorne Edge, doesn't he – the roughest estate in Barfax. There's a houseful of kids and the father's only a labourer at the lamp factory. They're probably living on about two hundred quid a week and yet this lad's taking you in wine-bars and treating you to Chinese meals. Where's he getting the money from, eh?'

'He gets up at six every morning and delivers papers. He's ace to be with, and it's not his fault if they haven't much money, is it?'

'Oh, I don't know, dear,' her mother said. 'That sort of family brings misfortune on itself, I always think. I mean – why have all those children when you're poor? Nobody made them have them, did they – it's not as if they were Catholics or anything.'

'Maybe they like children, Mum. Maybe if you and Dad liked children, I'd have brothers and sisters and you'd have better things to do with your time than polish your ornaments and spy on me. That's all I am to you, isn't it: just another of your rotten ornaments?'

She'd blown it, of course, and so here she was – banished to her room like a Jane Austen heroine. Except that Jane Austen heroines tend to obey their parents and Debbie wouldn't. Not this time. No chance.

5

Debbie is fourteen. Her parents don't spoil her but they fuss a lot, because she's all they've got. 'Now mind you stay with the group,' her mother says, whenever Debbie goes out in the evening.

One evening in 1970, Debbie's mother had left the group and encountered a rather coarse boy on a motorcycle while taking a short-cut over waste ground. What followed had been both exciting and terrifying and Debbie's mother had never forgotten it.

If Debbie's parents had their way, their daughter would never go out at all. She would sit in their spotless front room, doing her homework and watching suitable programmes on television. Suitable programmes, mind. Debbie's parents are born again Christians.

Debbie will never know that her father's mother was a drunken, foul-mouthed widow who kept a filthy house and entertained men in it. Debbie's mother does not know this, any more than her husband knows about the coarse boy on the motorcycle. Nobody knows all of anybody's secrets. Ever. And this is just as well. Debbie's parents would be appalled if they knew all of Debbie's.

So. Debbie's parents do what they can to protect her but, though she is something of an ornament to them – she was right about that – you can't keep a child in a glass case, and very soon now, as she takes her chance with the world like everybody else, they might even end up losing her.

6

Saturday afternoon. Eleven minutes before kick-off. Brian laid his eight pounds fifty down and pushed his way through the turnstile. It was dry and warm and the Kop was filling up. There was plenty of room though;

they never got much more than six thousand at Hillside, even on days like this.

Brian looked across the mass of green and white scarves and caps to the spot where he always stood with his friends. Colin must have been watching for him because he raised an arm and waved, shouting something Brian didn't catch. He began threading his way towards them.

It was the first league match of the season and they were all there: Colin, Lee, Jeannette, and Colin's brother Jonathan. 'Hey up, tatty-head!' grinned Colin, snatching at Brian's cap. Brian ducked, clamping his hands to his head.

'Where's Debbie?' asked Jeannette slyly.

'She's not coming. She doesn't mix with rubbish.'

'What's she going out with you for then?'

They mucked about, passing the time till kick-off; happy in anticipation of a new season, ripe with possibilities. The visiting side trotted out and loosened up by punting balls about. Their goalie swung briefly on the crossbar at the cowshed end, drawing chants of *'Oo it's a monkey'* from the home fans.

'Who are this lot anyway?' Jonathan asked.

'What you here for if you don't know that?' sneered Lee.

'Hull City,' Colin told him. 'They finished fourth last season.'

'They'll get murdered today,' said Lee with relish. 'Murdered.'

Barfax Town ran on to the pitch, waving. The crowd roared. From the cowshed rose a familiar chant. Brian grinned. The Ointment were in fine fettle as usual, swaying and showing their scarves. Two policemen moved round and stood with their hands clasped behind them, gazing up through the barrier as the Town fanatics swayed and sang.

'Why are they called the Ointment?' Jeannette asked.

Brian shrugged. 'Dunno.'

'You don't know nothing, man,' mocked Colin. 'D'you know what's warm and yellow and smells like bananas?'

'No.'

'Monkey sick.'

'Yech you mucky pig!'

''Course, you'll know all about that, won't you, Colin?' taunted Jeannette. 'You lot live on bananas, don't you?'

'Oh are you listenin', mister race relations man?' cried Colin. 'Pickin' on me just 'cause I's black. I could get you fifteen years for that, girl.'

'Naff off, Colin.'

The referee's whistle put a stop to the banter as the visitors kicked off. At once, the Ointment started to sing *We're gonna win the league.* Brian smiled again.

'Listen to 'em. Five seconds into the season and we're gonna win the league.'

22

'Well,' Lee retorted, 'we haven't given away any goals yet, have we?'

It was a cautious first half, as the two sides guarded their territory and tested each other with tentative thrusts. Nobody wants to lose the first match of the season. When the half-time whistle blew, neither side had opened its account. Colin treated the players to a baleful stare as they trooped off the field.

'Crap.'

Lee nodded gloomily. 'I thought Town'd be three up against these tossers by now. They would be and all, if they'd dump Harris and give Paxman a game.'

Colin shook his head. 'Bomber's all right. It's the others that want kicking into touch – especially that Rickstraw. A hundred thousand he cost 'em, and he couldn't run if his arse was on fire.'

'Give over moaning, you two,' said Jeannette. 'It's early days yet. We'll stuff 'em in the second half, no danger.'

On the field, a troupe of majorettes was performing. Jeannette nudged Lee and nodded towards Brian, who was watching them. 'Brian's into majorettes, y'know. It's the little skirts. He fancies that one with the baton.'

'Shut your gob,' growled Brian without turning. 'She's about ten – just right for you, Colin, kid.'

Colin grinned. 'Who you tryin' to kid, man? I seen you and her the other night down by the canal, holding hands. You sat on that wall with the no-cycling notice on it. You didn't see me on the other side, having a slash. You were telling her you love her. I went home and wrote a letter to Debbie. She'll get it Monday.'

Jeannette rolled her eyes. 'Ooo heck – I wouldn't be you at school Tuesday, Brian. She'll duff you up and tell everybody you're a cradle-snatcher. There'll be no hiding-place.'

'I reckon it was Brian did that Janet Stobbs in,' said Jonathan.

'Hey!' This time Brian did turn, and he wasn't smiling. 'You belt up about that, kiddo. That's not summat to make jokes about. What if it'd been Jeannette, eh?'

Jonathan flushed. 'I were only joking,' he mumbled. 'Everyone else were having you on, weren't they?' His eyes flicked from face to face, but nobody was backing him up. He looked down.

'Brian's right, Jonathan,' said Jeannette. 'There's some things you don't joke about. Anyway,' she brightened, 'what we talking about stuff like that for? Let's rip our programmes up and chuck 'em in the air when the lads come out.'

Janet Stobbs lies under a mound of raw yellow clay in Ferncliffe Cemetery. She's been there three weeks but that's nothing compared to the time she'll remain there. The wreaths and sprays are fading already, like people's memories of her. You can see the rusty wire between the stems.

Janet was twelve. Her mum used to warn her against accepting lifts from strangers, so she didn't. She accepted one from somebody she knew; somebody who always had a smile for her when they passed each other on the street.

Janet's mum weeps every night in bed, thinking about Janet and how she used to say woosh for shoes when she was two. She wonders – oh, how she wonders – why her little girl got into that car after all the warnings she'd received, and where the driver is now. She wants to kill that driver, and if she knew he slept soundly each night less than a mile away, she'd do it.

Debbie tossed a tube of toothpaste in the basket and headed for the checkout. It was Saturday afternoon and the supermarket was packed. She looked along the line, spotted the shortest queue and joined it. There were only four in front of her, but one had his trolley so full he'd survive two years on a desert island on its contents.

'Pig,' muttered Debbie. 'There's people starving in Africa.'

She was twelve minutes getting through. Staggering towards the exit with four bulging carriers, she felt a tap on her shoulder and turned to find Royston Ambler grinning at her. Royston was nineteen. His dad owned the lamp factory and was a millionaire. He was something important at the football club too. Debbie blushed. 'You'll develop arms like a gibbon lugging that lot home,' he said. 'Let me help you.'

'No, it's all right, thanks. My dad's outside with the car.'

'Oh. Well, at least I can carry a couple of bags out for you, can't I?'

'Yes. Thanks. Can you take one from each hand?'

'Sure.' He took the carriers and stood, looking at her. 'How about coming out for a drink with me tonight?'

She shook her head. 'I can't. I'm washing my hair. Anyway I don't drink.'

'Tomorrow night, then. A movie, not a drink.'

'I can't. I'm only fourteen, you know.'

'So what?'

'Well – you're eighteen or nineteen, aren't you? Isn't fourteen a bit young?'

'I'm nineteen, and fourteen isn't too young. Why should it be? I've got a car,' he added, as though this might make a difference.

Debbie shook her head. 'No, I'm sorry. I wouldn't feel right. You don't have to carry the bags if you don't want.'

He laughed. 'Of course I'll carry the bags. No hard feelings. I'll just have to keep trying, that's all.'

'Yes,' she said, and immediately wished she hadn't. Jesus, what a stupid thing to say. Her cheeks felt hot and she was confused. He was good-looking, and she knew several girls who were crazy about him, but he was definitely too old for her. She felt as though everyone in the supermarket was staring at her.

'Come on.' She walked out to the car and he followed a metre behind, like a servant or a porter or something. She felt mean about turning him down.

Her dad had seen them coming and was opening the boot. As they came up he smiled at Royston and said, 'Who's this, Deborah?'

'Ambler,' said Royston with a grin. 'Royston Ambler. I'm a friend of your daughter's. I saw her struggling and leapt to her assistance.'

Mr Baxter took the carriers from him and stowed them in the boot. 'Seth Ambler's lad?'

'That's right.'

'Well, it's very kind of you, Royston. Very kind. I didn't realize our Debbie knew you. Can we drop you anywhere?'

'Oh, no thanks, I've got the car.' He smiled at Debbie. 'I'll see you later, then.'

When he'd gone, Baxter said, 'I didn't know you and young Ambler were friends, Deb.'

Debbie shook her head. 'We're not. I've seen him around once or twice, that's all. He's good-looking though, isn't he?'

Her father smiled. 'He seems like a grand lad to me, love. His dad's an important figure in Barfax, too. Anyway, we'd best be off and pick your mother up.' They got into the car, and Baxter drove carefully out into the Saturday afternoon traffic.

9

The clock over the stand showed three fifty-nine. The majorettes marched off to a ripple of applause and the teams took the field again.

'Come on now, Town!' yelled Lee. 'Or we'll make you play the majorettes.'

Town kicked off and, with three fast, accurate passes and a glorious header from striker Harris, went ahead before Hull got a touch of the ball.

'Wee-yow!' screeched Lee. 'They must've heard me.' Harris, grinning, trotted towards the centre circle with his arms up and a knot of back-slapping team-mates round him. In the cowshed the Ointment stabbed the air with mocking fingers and serenaded the visiting supporters. *One nil, one nil, one nil, one nil.*

The Hull fans responded with *Sing when you're winning, you only sing when you're winning—*

Two minutes later winger Rickstraw ran the length of the field and crossed for Harris to nod home his second, and after that it was one-way traffic. When the final whistle blew, Town had four in the bag and goalie MacNee had kept a clean sheet.

'Oh yeah!' cried Colin. He turned to the others, his eyes shining. 'Come on – let's get the Hull coaches!'

'No.' Brian grabbed his friend's arm. 'Listen, Colin – we did em four–nil. They're going to be pig sick all the way home. We don't need to do owt else to 'em, do we?'

Colin looked at his friend. 'Y'know, Brian – you're an anorak. A real anorak. I never knew.' The others tittered and Brian felt himself go red.

The players were leaving the field. As they approached the tunnel a stout figure appeared on the balcony above it and clapped them in.

'Hey look,' said Jeannette. 'It's fatty Ambler. He thinks he's Alex Ferguson or summat, just 'cause he got Rickstraw. He probably only got him 'cause nobody else wanted him.'

When the last player had disappeared down the tunnel, Ambler gripped the guard rail with both hands and stood gazing out across the stadium. As Chairman of Barfax Town AFC he felt entitled to regard this place as his empire. His only empire, now. Until this week there had been the lamp factory too, which he had inherited from his father and in which a high proportion of the people of Barfax was employed, including some of the parents of the little knot of youngsters who lingered on the Kop and appeared to be watching him. Now the factory was going and there was only this. He experienced a rare glow of pleasure at the thought. He smiled.

'Captain sodding Bligh,' said Lee. 'Watching someone get flogged.'

'Knickers to him,' growled Colin. 'We won, didn't we? Come on.' They formed a conga-line and began capering diagonally across the Kop, chanting *'We won, cha-cha-cha; we won, cha-cha-cha.'*

Ambler watched them. The words of the chant came faintly to his ears. He smiled again. 'Aye, we won,' he told himself as he went back into the box. 'That's all their sort cares about.'

10

When Brian got back from the match, there was news.

'Guess what – our Carole's got a flat.'

'You needn't sound so flippin' pleased about it, Mick,' reproved his mother, slamming a panful of burgers on the table.

'And it's not a flat neither,' said Carole, struggling to get a bib on Nicholas. 'It's a room. A bedsit. It's nowt brilliant but it'll do for now.'

Brian draped his scarf and cap over a chair-back. He looked at his sister. 'Where is it?'

'Venn Street. One of them big houses. A lot of students live round there.'

'Aye, I know,' grunted Brian. 'And a lot of winos and weirdos and criminals and all. You'll have to watch it, our Carole; the feller that did that girl in probably lives round there.'

'Will you shut up?' Carole shivered. 'Anyway, I want you to come round with me after tea and carry some stuff up.'

'I can't. I'm meeting Debbie. You're never moving tonight?'

'Why not – there isn't room for us here, is there?'

'Well, no. But—'

'Well, then. Dad's running us round after tea. It's furnished, so there's not a lot to take, but I thought it'd be easier with three, that's all.'

Brian shrugged. 'Yeah, well – if it's straight after tea I can – I don't meet Debbie till seven. Whose flat is it?'

'A Paki's.' Dale had come into the room and intercepted the question. 'She's rented a room off a Paki. That's why I'm not helping her. She should've waited and got one off a white man.'

'Why?' asked Brian. 'What difference does it make? A room's a room and a landlord's a landlord. I just wish it wasn't in Venn Street.'

'Come and get your teas.' Their mother set down a bowlful of chips and a plate of bread and butter. 'Where's your dad?'

'Outside,' said Dale. 'Doing summat to t'car.'

'Go tell him his tea's ready.'

Dale left the room. The others took their places round the table.

'He didn't want me to have it.' Carole was bending over the baby's chair, cutting up chips for the child.

'How d'you mean?'

'He didn't want me to have it. He kept saying "It is no good for you – it is room for a man. It is not room for a young lady."' She laughed and sat down. 'I said to him, "Look: I've got a baby. Nobody wants you when you've got a baby. I've got to have the room." So in the end he took me up and showed me. Like I said, it's nowt special but it's all right.' She turned to the child, dabbing his mouth with a corner of the bib. 'We'll manage, won't we, mucktub – you and me?'

Brian looked down at his plate. We've pushed her out, he thought. All of us. Out of the house and out of the family. She knows we don't want her and so she's off to live in Venn Street with the other unwanted folk.

He recalled a night months ago when he'd walked along Venn Street on his way home from a party. He'd seen three drunks sitting on a low wall under some rampant privet, drinking cider. He'd crossed the street, walking with his head down: watching them out of his eye corner. Two men, and a shape-less woman in a man's overcoat who seemed to have wet herself. These three, or others like them, would be his sister's neighbours now.

A sudden ache filled his throat, and to his horror he felt tears in his eyes. He ducked his head and wiped them with his sleeve. Luckily, Dale and his father chose that moment to come in, and nobody seemed to notice.

As soon as the meal was over, Carole and Brian went upstairs to get Carole's things together while their mother got the baby ready. In the bedroom, Carole laid a hand on her brother's arm.

'Hey listen: it's all right y'know. I'll be all right.'

He flushed, knowing she'd seen him crying. 'I know.' He looked at the floor. 'It's just – well, it's like we've pushed you out.'

'You haven't, silly – I wanted me and Nick to have a place of our own. We're a family, see? A separate family. OK?'

He nodded. 'Yeah. Only you're not unwanted, Carole. That's what I mean. Not like some of them round Venn Street.'

'Oh, Brian!' She gave him a brief, exasper-ated hug. 'I know that, love.' She pushed him out to arm's length and looked into his face. 'You always were the soft one of the family, weren't you?'

He nodded again, biting his lip. Carole

dropped her hands. 'Come on,' she said briskly. 'Dad's waiting.'

They carried things down in suitcases, cardboard boxes, and dustbin bags and loaded them in the back of the old banger. Brian and his mother squeezed in the back among all the stuff and Carole sat in front with the baby on her knee. 'I'll have to call in for the key,' she said. 'It's a shop. I'll show you.'

They drove through the estate and out along the ring-road. It was a warm, late summer evening. Brian gazed out of the window at quiet streets and dusty sunshine. In an hour it would be dusk, and these streets would be alive with people, off to make the most of Saturday night. He wondered if Carole ever wished she could still do that. 'Course she does, he told himself. She must do.

The shop was an off-licence at the corner of Cornwall Terrace and Venn Street. Dad stopped the car and took the baby from Carole. She got out. Brian climbed over some of her belongings and got out too. She gave him a wan smile.

'There's no need, Brian. I shan't be a tick.'

'I wanted to see him, that's all. Go on.'

She went into the shop and he followed her. It was dim inside, and cool. There was a strong smell of paraffin. A plump Pakistani woman came through a bead curtain. When she saw Carole she smiled, said something in her own language and went back through the curtain.

A moment later a thin, moustachioed man appeared.

'Ah.' He smiled briefly at Carole, then turned and spoke to Brian. 'You – are with this young lady?'

Brian nodded. 'She's my sister.'

'Ah. Then perhaps—' He made a helpless gesture with his palms. 'I have told her – I have tried to explain that my rooms are for men only. They are not nice rooms, you understand. Rough people live there. Noisy people. Sometimes, there is trouble.'

Brian nodded. 'I know, but she needs a place. She says your room suits her, so there's nothing I can do. She's nineteen.'

'Nineteen, yes.' The man looked unhappy. 'Well – I will give you the key. Go with her to the room and you will see. Bring it back if you want to. I do not mind.' He pulled a fist-sized bunch of keys from his pocket and detached one. 'Here.' He gave it to Brian. 'You will not want your sister in such a room.'

They left the shop. Their parents were watching through the car window. Carole pointed along the street and called, 'It's just there, Dad. Nineteen, this side. Drive on – me and our Brian might as well walk.' Her father wound down the window.

'What?'

'Drive on. Number nineteen. We'll walk.'

'Righto.'

They walked along the cracked, uneven

pavement while the car lurched over the setts in a haze of exhaust. Brian looked at the houses. Some had been painted in clashy, garish colours; the paint slapped on anyhow so that brickwork and window-panes were spattered. Others hadn't seen a lick of paint since the war. Dirty lace curtains sagged in streaky windows and the tiny strips of garden lay sour under rampant couch-grass and privet gone wild. Mattresses and the skeletons of push-chairs mouldered in the tangle.

Number nineteen had a green door framed in mauve, and orange window-frames.

There was a clean patch on the stonework where somebody had tried to scrub out a large, sprayed-on swastika.

'Well,' said Carole brightly. 'This is it, kiddo.'

'Jesus,' said Brian. 'The guy who painted this needs help.'

Mum and Dad clambered out of the car, Mum carrying the baby and looking upset. 'Your mum doesn't like the look of this, Carole,' said Dad.

'No, I can see that.' Carole smiled at her mother. 'Why don't you sit in the car with Nick, Mum? You can't do owt anyway, with him in your arms.'

The older woman looked at the windows. 'Which is yours?'

'You can't see it from here, Mum. It's round the back.'

'Aye, and I bet it's even more of a mess than this lot round the front.' She looked at her daughter. 'We can keep you with us a bit longer, love – till summat nice comes up.'

Carole laughed, shaking her head. 'Summat nice'll never come up, Mum – not for a lass on her own with a kid. Wait in the car, eh?'

They trotted, the three of them, up and down a flight of creaky stairs with armfuls of Carole's things till the car was empty and the little room was full. When it was done, Carole came down with them to get the baby and say goodbye to her mother.

'Don't look like that, Mum; we'll be all right, honest.'

'There's a good strong bolt on the inside of the door,' put in Dad. 'She's promised to keep it on at night, haven't you, love?' Carole nodded.

'I'm off up now. The sun's gone and Nick'll catch cold.' She took the child from her mother. 'Listen – we'll pop round for tea tomorrow. OK?'

They watched till she turned in the doorway and waved. Then they got in the car and drove back along Venn Street. Looking back, Brian saw the little shopkeeper on his doorstep, staring after them.

Carole came for Sunday tea, as she'd said she would. Everybody fussed over her and played with the kid as though they hadn't seen them for months. Brian marvelled at this phenomenon. They'd shifted Dale's bed into her old room, and he had had to admit to himself that it was nice to have the space, and to know there'd be no more broken nights.

They'd come on the bus, but when it was time to go Dad ran them back in the car. Everybody except Dale stood on the step and waved them off. Dale, still brooding over the colour of his sister's landlord, had kept himself to himself all afternoon and retired to the lavatory when Carole started putting Nick's coat on.

The visit left Brian feeling better. His sister had seemed cheerful enough. She was still one of the family and Venn Street was only a bus ride away.

Monday was the last day of the holidays. Brian and Debbie had arranged to meet, but her parents decided to be awkward and by the time she got to the arcade, Brian had been walking about for half an hour trying not to look at his watch.

'I'm sorry, love,' she said. 'It wasn't easy to get away. They made me get all my stuff ready for school. I'd to iron a blouse and skirt and

Mum's always done them before. I think they knew I was coming to see you.'

Brian shrugged. 'Don't worry. I'm just glad you made it. What the heck they got against me anyway?'

'Oh.' She smiled wryly. 'They think big families who live in council houses are all criminals. And you're a hooligan because you follow Town.'

'Maybe I am.'

She laughed. 'No, you're not. A pig and a bore yes, but not a hooligan. What shall we do?'

'I don't know. I've got nowt as usual.'

'Surprise surprise.'

'We could go for a walk.'

'Big deal. No, listen. I've got nine fifty and I'm starving. Why don't we go down the Chicken Shack?'

Brian pulled a face. 'Our Mick'll be there. And anyway it's rat. He told me.'

'Knickers. There's no wings on a rat.'

'Did I say rat? I meant bat.'

'Stupid! Come on.'

They left the arcade and walked along holding hands. It was early for the Chicken Shack and the place was empty. The manageress didn't work Mondays and Mick was in charge. He came to the counter and played the game of pretending they were strangers.

'Yes?'

'Bat and chips twice please,' said Brian.

'Sorry, sir. We're right out of bats. Waiting for delivery. We've got some slugs, though.'

At the back of the shop a teenage girl was loading chips into a wire basket. She was pretending to concentrate on her task but Brian, watching over his brother's shoulder, could tell she was listening. He hadn't seen her before and guessed she was new. He wondered what she was thinking. Debbie, crimson with suppressed laughter, was keeping Mick between herself and the girl.

'What are they like, slugs?'

'Our more discerning customers tell us they resemble scampi, sir.'

'We'll have some then. Two scoops, with chips.'

Mick turned and called to the girl. 'Fetch us a carton of slugs up, love.'

'Eh?' The girl put down the basket of chips and gazed at him, open-mouthed.

'Slugs,' he repeated. 'In the cellar. By the oil.' Mick was one of those people who can keep a straight face no matter what the situation.

The girl started for the cellar, then hesitated. She was new, and desperately wanted to do the right thing, and yet— 'Slugs?' she queried. 'You mean like you get in t'garden?'

'Aye,' said Mick, patiently. 'Like you get in t'garden. Go on then.'

Still she hesitated. Conviction and doubt struggled for possession of her features.

Finally she shook her head, uttered an odd little mew and disappeared through the door that led to the cellar steps.

Debbie collapsed against the counter laughing while Mick, poker-faced, wiped the top with a damp cloth. 'Poor lass!' hooted Brian. 'You should've seen her face when you said you were out of bats. How long's she been here?'

'She only started this morning,' Mick told him. 'She's called Tracy. She won't last long. Nobody does. It's killing work when you're busy and deadly boring when you're not. And you've no social life because you're working when everybody else is playing.'

'You stuck.'

'Oh aye – but I'm not all that bothered about going out. I shan't be here much longer anyway, unless Doreen moves on and they make me manager. They use kids so they don't have to pay owt. As soon as you're eighteen and start wanting a proper wage, they fire you and get another kid. There's thousands waiting, you see, and anybody can do the work.'

'Pillocks,' said Brian. 'We shouldn't be laughing really. Go tell her we were having her on, eh?'

There was no need. Tracy had heard the laughter and was standing, pink-faced, in the doorway. She shot Mick a reproachful glare. 'What you want to do that for?'

Mick grinned at her. 'Everybody winds up the new girl,' he said, 'or the new boy. It's sort of tradition. Doreen sent me out for some soup-knives my first week. I went, and all.'

'Hmm!' Tracy wasn't to be mollified that easily. She gave them a baleful stare, tossed her head and went back to loading chips. Mick shrugged and turned to his customers. 'What d'you really want – or did you just come to gaze upon my devilishly handsome features?'

'Handsome?' scoffed Brian. 'You're about as handsome as a vulture's crutch. We want two pieces and chips twice, and Debbie's paying.'

Mick shook his head. 'Nobody's paying. Staff's allowed two-and-chips, but when you've been handling 'em all day you can't fancy them. They knock 'em off your wage whether you eat them or not, so you might as well have mine and Tracy's.' He turned. 'OK, Trace?'

'Spect so.'

Deftly, Mick made up the two packs and slid them across the counter. 'There y'are – on the house.'

'Lovely!' Brian scooped them up and handed one to Debbie.

'Thanks, Mick.' He looked across to where the girl was jiggling a basket of chips about in the pan. 'See you, Tracy.'

'OK.' She didn't look up.

They walked and ate, leaving the busy road where the Chicken Shack stood to saunter through a quiet, leafy suburb. The houses here were large, stone-built places with neat lawns and garages for two or even three cars. After a while they stopped under a horse-chestnut tree and stood with bones in their fists, stripping off shreds of flesh with their teeth and gazing up a gravelled driveway.

'Mum and Dad want to move here,' said Debbie.

Brian spat out a fragment of gristle. 'I bet they do.'

'They're saving. I hope they don't make it till I've left home. The kids around here are bound to be toffee-nosed gits with ponies who go to private schools.'

'They don't let ponies go to private schools.'

'Idiot. You know what I mean.'

'Yeah.' He nipped the last sliver of meat from a legbone and dropped it in the box. 'You finished?'

'Just about.'

They put the boxes on the grass and wiped their mouths and fingers with the moist paper napkins provided. Then they balled up the napkins and dropped them among the bones. Brian picked up both boxes and they walked on, turning into Duchy Drive. Halfway along was a particularly imposing house with a white-railed balcony, immaculate lawns and neatly clipped hedges of beech and yew. Brian threw the boxes over the hedge. They burst on impact, scattering chicken-bones and scraps of paper on the lawn. Debbie gave him a half-disapproving look.

'Maybe you are a hooligan after all.'

'No I'm not. I'm a terrorist. The phantom bomber of Duchy Drive.'

'You're awful.'

'Could be worse. As my campaign intensifies, I might start creeping up driveways to pee through letter-boxes.'

'Pig. I think we'd better get out of here.'

They spent the rest of the day lounging around the park, avoiding company, but when Debbie mentioned Saturday and Brian told her he was off to Bournemouth with the Town travel club, they quarrelled.

'Bournemouth?' Her expression was incredulous. 'That's nearly three hundred miles away. Who the heck wants to travel three hundred miles just to watch a rotten football match?'

'I do. Me and about four hundred others. There's three coaches going, and there'll be loads going by car and train. You want to come with us, love – it'll be great.'

'I do not! You're barmy, the lot of you. What time d'you have to set off?'

'Half six, from in front of the Norfolk Gardens. It's only seventeen quid. I'll pay for you if you like.'

'No way. Where would you get thirty-four pounds from?'

'Saved up. I've enough for every away fixture.'

'No wonder you'd nowt on you today, you cheeky bugger.'

He grinned. 'You don't mind spending your brass on a good-looking fella like me, do you? I spend plenty on you when I've got it, don't I?'

'Depends what you mean by plenty. Royston Ambler'd spend more and he's got a car and all.'

'Royston Ambler?' It was Brian's turn to be incredulous. 'Royston Ambler's nineteen and his dad's a millionaire. He wouldn't even look at you.'

'He does do. He's asked me out.'

'You're joking.'

Debbie shook her head. 'He asked me in Sainsbury's.'

'The mucky old cradle-snatcher. What did you say?'

'I told him I was too young for him.'

'And what did he say?'

'He said fourteen's fine, or something like that.'

'Aye. He would. He's a wally, Deb. A creep.'

'He's quite good-looking, and at least he won't talk about flippin' football all the time. I might even take him up on his offer one of these Saturdays when you're off to Bournemouth or Torquay or somewhere.'

'Suit yourself, but you could be wrong about the football – his dad's Chairman at Hillside, y'know.'

'He doesn't go.'

'Maybe he doesn't get on with his dad. Anyway you go out with him if you want, but I don't think much of your taste.'

It wasn't a heated quarrel but it spoilt the day, and when Brian saw Debbie home at nine they parted on the corner without kissing. Brian stood watching till she was safely inside, then shrugged and turned for home. She was all right, old Deb. They'd make it up at school tomorrow. She'd be over it by then.

12

Tuesday September third at five past nine. The school hall. Old Dodgson on the platform, holding his lapels like something out of an Edwardian photo and frowning down at the new kids at the front.

'Standards,' he intoned, and a faint groan arose in the ranks. Brian shuffled a couple of centimetres to his left in order to be able to see the back of Debbie's head three rows in front. Here we go again, folks. Standards. If we succeed in teaching you nothing else, I am determined that each one of you will leave this school with an awareness of the importance of standards. Blah, blah, blah. Some of the groaning had come from the staff.

Debbie had cut him dead in the yard. Spun on her heel and walked off with her nose in the air, just because he was off to Bournemouth Saturday. Daft cow.

Bournemouth. A tingle of anticipation prickled his scalp. Roll on Saturday. The Town'll crucify 'em. Bound to. Far better side. Standards, you see. That's what it's all about. Dodgson knows.

Straight after assembly, Brian's group had to endure another load of crap, this time from Ramsden. At least they could listen to it sitting down. Dead keen, Ramsden was. If Dodgson's buzz-word was standards, Ramsden's was qualifications. It is impossible to get anywhere these days without qualifications. He meant GCSEs. I left school without qualifications, and I was not an unqualified success. Ha, ha, flippin' ha. Big joke, except when you've heard it thirty-six thousand times before. It is impossible to get anywhere these days, period. How many qualifications do you need to draw benefit?

Ramsden went on to tell them how he came to realize the importance of qualifications, and how he had to be in night school studying for his O-levels while his mates were out

supping and chasing lasses.
heart, same as always. Sometin
he wasn't in the top set. It'd be a l
if he was with Lee and Colin. The dea
as Ramsden called them. They spent a
time outside school: visiting places, inter-
viewing people on the street and counting
traffic. Stuff like that. And people came into
school to talk to them about shopping and
filling in forms and looking after babies. It was
great. A doddle. And they got practically no
homework, so who were the real fools, eh?

'We expect great things of you,' Ramsden
was saying. 'Great things. And you are
capable of great things – each one of you. If
you were not, you wouldn't be in this set. But
let there be no mistake; it will entail hard
work: plenty of hard work from you, and even
harder work by me.'

'I bet,' muttered Brian. 'Sitting there picking
your nails, trying to decide whether to play a
round of golf tonight or stuff yourself rotten
in some posh restaurant.'

He didn't fancy the year ahead. Make or
break year, Ramsden had called it. He knew
what that meant. Homework. Piles of it.
Revision. Tests. Notes from Ramsden to his
parents, telling them how well he might do if
only he would apply himself. He'd already
been on at him to give up his paper round. Fat
chance. All this, and no brass in his pocket?
That'll be the day.

refused to speak to him all that first week, and he walked home each afternoon with Lee and Colin. He didn't know who Debbie walked with, and he told himself he didn't care.

PART TWO

QUE SERA, SERA . . .

1

Saturday dawned blustery and cool. It was lie-in morning for the Gower household and Brian tiptoed about, getting his stuff together and grabbing a bit of breakfast. Brian had persuaded the newsagent he delivered for to find a stand-in just this once. It hadn't gone down too well, but the man had agreed in the end. At ten to six he slipped out of the house and set off for town, his green and white scarf flapping in the wind.

When he arrived in front of the hotel, the others were already there. Jonathan was wearing a gigantic rosette. Brian fingered it. 'Where the heck d'you get this thing, kiddo? It's like a flamin' dustbin-lid.'

'My mum made me it. What's up with it?'

'Nowt's up with it,' said Colin. 'Ignore him, our kid – he's only jealous.'

'I'm not jealous, you wassock – he looks like a rat behind a cartwheel.'

Fans were arriving all the time. Some carried plastic carriers or sports bags full of drinks and sandwiches. All wore scarves or bobble-caps or both. Soon, the pavement in front of the hotel was crammed with Town supporters. Most were youths and boys, with a sprinkling of girls and older people. A solitary policeman, pasty-faced from a night on the beat, treated the assembly to a suspicious stare as he passed by.

At twenty past six the three coaches swung into view. There was a ragged cheer. Patsy Dillinger, secretary of the travel club, stepped forward and started getting people organized. When everybody was on board it was discovered that three people hadn't turned up. Patsy insisted on giving them five minutes but they didn't come, and at twenty-five to seven the coaches pulled out and headed for the motorway, scarves streaming from their windows.

The journey was exhilarating but largely uneventful. Songs were sung, Coke cans drained and left to roll about the floor, sandwiches eaten. Somewhere near Birmingham they pulled into a service area and invaded the lavatories, shouting, laughing and jostling. Barry Weatherall sprayed the word Ointment on the wall then led his comrades in a sweep of the entire establishment, seeking rival fans. There were none.

They entered Bournemouth at a quarter to one, and by five past the three coaches were parked in a narrow street near the football ground. Both ends of this street were coned off and policemen and -women, some on horses, patrolled watchfully. Two dog vans stood nearby.

Brian looked out. Patsy Dillinger was talking to a police inspector. After a minute he climbed into the coach and held up a hand for silence.

'Right, lads.' He spotted Jeannette. 'And lasses. There was a lot of bother with fans at this ground last year, and the police aren't letting us off till half an hour before kick-off. That means we've got to sit here for—' He looked at his watch. 'An hour and twenty minutes.'

Boos, groans, and catcalls greeted this announcement and Patsy raised his hand again. 'I know, I know – we've been over six hours getting here and you're all stiff and fed-up. I pointed this out to the inspector but he says there's nothing he can do. However, there are some toilets round the corner and if we get up a party of those who want to go he'll arrange an escort.'

'Wheeee!' cried Lee. 'A bog-party. Who's coming?'

Everybody went. The police split them into batches and the batches took turns. By the time everybody was back in the coaches, there was less than an hour to go.

The time passed slowly after that but it passed, and at twenty-five past two they left the coaches and began walking towards the ground. Mounted police rode along the pavement-edge, confining the Town supporters to one side of the road. From the other side, where Bournemouth fans trudged along beyond a line of parked cars, came whistles, catcalls, and the occasional missile.

Brian and his friends reached the turnstiles, laid down their money and passed into the ground. The Town fans had been allocated a section of the terraces. High, steel-mesh double barriers prevented any direct contact with the home crowd, but as the visitors streamed in, home supporters pressed up to the barriers, chanting '*Eh bah goom*' (clap-clap-clap) '*Eh bah goom*' (clap-clap-clap).

'Listen at 'em,' growled Colin. 'Thick southern gits.'

'Sod 'em,' said Lee. 'They won't be singing at half-time when they're three down.'

They found a vantage-point halfway between the turnstiles and the barrier. The Ointment, led by Barry Weatherall, went and stood as close to the mesh as they could. They hooked their fingers through it, rattling it and making hideous faces across the strip of no man's land. A constable ran down the strip with his truncheon drawn. Weatherall and the others withdrew their fingers, contenting themselves with jeers and raspberries till he had gone.

Barfax appeared in their green and white strip, drawing jeers from the home crowd. Goalkeeper MacNee trotted across, waving to the Town contingent who responded with applause. A toilet-roll arched through the air, unravelling. MacNee gathered it in and tossed it on the track. The crowd roared as the home team appeared.

Town won the toss and kicked off. After twenty minutes of good, end-to-end play, Foulds found Harris with a superb cross and, following a mistake by the keeper, the striker shot into the back of the net.

The Barfax fans leapt, cheered, and waved their scarves at their dejected rivals. Lee grabbed Jeannette and they spun, laughing in each other's faces. 'Told you!' crowed Lee. 'Three by half-time.'

The game continued, but there was to be no feast of goals. Barfax, having achieved the lead, fell back and defended it and the score was unchanged at half-time.

Jeannette looked at Lee. 'What happened to them other two goals then, Lee?'

'It's Harris,' said Lee. 'He's got a pointed head so most of his headers go wide. If he stood on his head and spun round he'd vanish into the ground.'

'Rubbish!' snarled Colin. 'Carries the flamin' side, old Bomber does. I've told you before – it's that Rickshaw they want shot of. He's too slow, man. A one hundred thousand pound pensioner, that's what he is.'

Away to their right, the Ointment were taunting the home fans. Aziz Khan leapt for the wire, clung to it and turned, yelling, 'A Cornish – give us a Cornish, quick!' Two policemen were running down the strip between the fences. A youth surrendered his pasty and Khan hurled it into the Bournemouth crowd. To the delight of his friends it hit a youth on the ear and burst, shooting hot mush down his neck. Gasping with pain, the youth hopped about, clawing the stuff from under his collar while the Ointment laughed.

'D'you see that?' cried Jeannette. 'If they had Cornish-chucking in t'Olympics, Aziz'd win gold.'

As the two policemen ran at him, Khan performed a backward leap off the barrier, but he was doomed to miss the second half of the match. Other policemen were closing in and, though his friends tried to hide him, he was seized and led away in an arm-lock with the cheers of the Ointment ringing in his ears.

'Daft sod,' grunted Colin. 'Three hundred miles to see half a match.'

Jeannette nodded. 'First half and all. And he'll probably get duffed up and fined a hundred quid.'

The teams trotted out. The home crowd stood virtually silent this time, while the Barfax contingent yelled itself hoarse. As Brian had prophesied, there were about four hundred of them. As their voices faded, a section of the Bournemouth crowd retaliated with *'Come in a taxi – you must have come in a taxi—'*

Bournemouth equalized two minutes into the second half, and this marked the beginning of a torrid spell for the Barfax defence as the home side piled on the pressure. It was gripping stuff, but Brian scarcely noticed it. He was thinking about the Ointment, and about the cries of acclamation which had followed Aziz Khan out of the ground. Daft sod, Colin had called him, and of course he was right. What's the point of spending seventeen pounds or more following your team away, only to be frogmarched off the ballpark before you know the outcome? How splendid, on the other hand, to belong to the Ointment; to be one of a hard elite, feared by all, and to be a hero in the eyes of your friends.

He recalled Colin's sneering words last week at Hillside. 'You're an anorak. A real anorak. I never knew.' He remembered how the others had sniggered. And then there was Carole saying 'You always were the soft one of the family.' Funny, he thought, how the remarks that hurt you most are always made by people you like.

He was roused from his brooding by the sudden, excited cries of those around him. Throwing everything forward, Bournemouth had been caught napping. Defender Cook had blocked a shot and lofted the ball out to Ham. The nippy winger had chested it down and was now streaking into the Bournemouth half with the home defence stranded.

The desperate keeper did the only thing he could, charging out in an attempt to narrow the angle. Ham waited till the big man was almost on him, then swerved round him and ran the ball into the empty net.

The remaining twenty-five minutes saw nonstop aggression by the home team and stubborn defence by Barfax. Bournemouth almost equalized following a corner in the eighty-ninth minute but the visitors held out, the final whistle being preceded by dozens from the lips of tense Town supporters.

'If we can go on playing like that away from home,' said Lee, 'we're up.'

There was a bit of congestion round the exit with the police anxious to keep the Barfax fans back till the home supporters had been dispersed. The Town fans were in high spirits, and after a few minutes of good-natured pushing and shoving they began streaming away from the ground, hemmed in as before by a high wall on one side and horses on the other.

The operation to disperse the Bournemouth fans had met with only partial success. As the visitors trudged chatting along the road, missiles began falling among them.

'Hey up.' A middle-aged man in front of Brian flinched and ducked as a stone whizzed past his head and bounced off the wall. 'They want to get them beggars sorted out – there's women and kids here.'

Across the road was some sort of park or

recreation ground. Laurel and rhododendron crowded up to its iron fence, and it was from among this overgrown shrubbery that the stones were coming. A couple of policemen dodged between moving cars and shinned over the fence, vanishing into the tangle.

'They'll never find 'em in that lot,' said Colin. 'Come on – let's get past.' He grabbed Jeannette and they half ran, crouching, shielding their heads with their arms. The others followed.

Brian, bringing up the rear, was almost out of danger when he heard a voice he recognized. 'Chicken,' it said. He looked over his shoulder and there they were – the Ointment, hands in pockets, making a big show of not being in a hurry. Barry Weatherall was gazing at him through mocking eyes. 'Chicken,' he repeated, softly. At that moment a large stone came skittering across the flags in front of Brian's feet. His cheeks burned with a mixture of rage and humiliation. He wanted to fling himself at Weatherall – to smash his fist into that mocking face until its expression of contempt became one of respect. Instead, he bent and picked up the stone. It wasn't a stone, but a lump of concrete. Gritting his teeth to control the shaking of his body, he glanced towards the line of crawling cars. Directly opposite was a yellow Citroën with a Bournemouth scarf trailing limply from its window.

It was like a sign – an omen. He knew at

once what he was supposed to do and he did it without hesitation. The missile struck the window with an explosive crack, shattering it. The driver braked sharply and the Citroën was hit by a Metro that had been following it.

Terror washed over Brian, but instinct told him he mustn't run. From behind came the cheers he had coveted but he didn't want them now. He slunk along, wanting only the anonymity of the crowd. At each moment he expected a hand to drop on his shoulder, but as the seconds passed it became clear that by some miracle, nobody in authority had seen him throw the stone. Somewhere behind, the driver was shouting. A mounted sergeant raked the throng with his eyes while constables on foot dodged about, calling to one another. Brian stuck his hands in his pockets and mooched along with his head down, whistling. Some metres in front of him walked Colin and the others. They had turned their heads in the direction of the noise when the stone had hit the car, but it certainly had not occurred to any of them that Brian might have thrown it. Behind him, he could hear the Ointment laughing and making remarks about him but it was not mocking laughter, and their remarks held the ring of approval.

As they neared the coaches, Brian's heartbeat slowed and he was able to think rationally about what he had done. He could scarcely credit that he had done it at all. It was like nothing he had ever done before in his life and he knew it was wrong, and yet now, with the danger of detection seemingly past, he remembered the cheers and a warm glow suffused his breast. They had cheered him – the Ointment had actually cheered Brian the anorak Gower and he liked it. He liked it so much that as soon as the coach was rolling he intended to share it with the others.

A knot of fans stood by the coach step, waiting patiently while an elderly man helped his rheumaticky wife on board. As Brian waited to get on, a heavy hand descended on his shoulder. He stiffened. His face drained of colour. Slowly, he turned his head. Barry Weatherall grinned down at him. 'Great shot, kid,' he growled, and moved on towards his own coach. Brian followed the hulking figure for a moment with his eyes, then turned and clambered on board to tell Colin.

2

When Barry Weatherall was six, he wet his pants one morning while struggling to read to the teacher. He was a big boy for his age but he couldn't learn to read. Everybody else had read at least four books, but Barry was stuck on Little Book One.

He wasn't called Barry in those days. He was called Nigel. Nigel Robert Weatherall. After he wet his pants the teacher grabbed him and dragged him out from behind her table so everyone could see him.

'Look, children!' she cried, crushing his wrist with bony, spiteful fingers. 'Look what this great big baby has done.' And she had held him there, at arm's length, with an expression of disgust on her prim face, until everybody had had a good laugh and slow, clumsy Nigel had dissolved into tears of humiliation.

A full year had been too short a time for Nigel to master reading, but he learned in a day how to win the respect of his peers. At playtime he tracked down those of his classmates who had laughed loudest and beat them up, with the result that, though the teacher referred in class to Nigel's little accident from time to time afterwards, nobody laughed. And when, a few years later, a boy at his middle school told him Nigel was a poncy name, Nigel knocked out most of his teeth as a way of demonstrating that you can't always go by names. Nevertheless, when he was fifteen he took to calling himself Barry, and it wasn't long before everybody else learned to call him Barry too.

So now it's Barry Weatherall, King of the Hillside Kop. He has long since forgotten the embarrassing incident when he was six.

The teacher died on a rubber sheet a few years ago, and if anybody else remembers they're not dumb enough to remind him. He's forgotten the incident, but not the lesson it taught him, which is that everybody's good at something, and the secret of success is to find out what you're good at and do it with all your might. He still doesn't read too well, but a lot of people follow him on Saturday afternoons and a lot more admire him from afar. And some of them can read quite well.

3

The coach stopped a couple of times on the way back and it was after eleven when Brian got home. His mother was watching the late film.

'We won,' he crowed, dropping his scarf on a chair. 'Two–one.'

'Aye, we know,' said Mum. 'We had *Grandstand* on. You've been a long time getting back.'

'We'd to wait for these two fellas. Every time the coach stopped they were late getting back on. There's always someone like that, but it was worth it, Mum. They played great. You should've . . .' He broke off as a heavy thump shook the house, followed at once by a screeching dragging noise.

'What's that?'

'Dale and your dad.'

'What they doing?'

She sighed. 'Shifting Dale's bed back into your room.'

'What the heck for?'

'Because Carole's back, that's why.'

'Eh? Where is she?'

'Upstairs, getting Nick settled.'

'What's up? I mean, what happened?'

'She's been broken into. Attacked.' His mother spoke quietly. 'She's not going back there any more.'

'Who attacked her – is she hurt?'

As he spoke there were footfalls on the stairs and his sister came into the room. She'd been crying.

'Who attacked you?' he demanded. She shook her head. 'He didn't attack me exactly. He didn't get a chance. He was drunk and he bust the door in. I screamed and someone from down the hall came in and grabbed him. He was just drunk but I can't go back. The noises late at night. That stinking lavatory. I'm not bringing my Nick up in a dump like that.'

'He told you – the landlord.'

'I know. But you don't know till you're there, do you? I was desperate for a place.'

'You don't have to be, love,' said her

mother. 'This is your home. We managed before and we'll manage again.'

This started Carole crying again. Her shoulders heaved and great, choking sobs came out of her. Brian felt uncomfortable. He always had, seeing older people crying. It was one of the reasons he detested funerals. To mask his discomfiture he said, 'Has Nick gone down all right?'

She nodded, sinking into a chair and pulling a tissue out of her sleeve. 'In his cot.' She sniffed, dabbing her cheeks with the tissue. 'In Mum's room. Dad and Dale are shifting Dale's bed back and putting mine up. You'd better go give them a hand.'

He got up, glad to escape from the room. When he got upstairs, the job was nearly finished. His dad looked irritable and Dale was muttering about lousy Pakis. Brian said nothing but pitched in and did what he could, helping with a mattress and humping blankets through. He was feeling pretty fed up himself. He realized that there was nothing Carole could have done in the circumstances except come home, but the extra space had been good and now, after only one week, it was gone.

He thought about the house on Duchy Drive, where he'd thrown his litter on the lawn. There'd be empty bedrooms in that house with dust-sheets over costly, unused furniture. It wasn't right. It was life, but it wasn't right. When they found his litter they probably tut-tutted and shook their heads and muttered about yobbos, without having the slightest idea of what life was like on Thorne Edge. They had it sussed, those people. Planned out, down to the last detail. They knew where they'd be next week, next month, next year at this time. Knew where the kids'd go to school and what they'd do after. Who they'd marry probably. Or at least that they'd marry well and be comfortable. They had no worries, people like them. Not real ones. Nobody chasing them for brass. Everything was foreseen and provided for in advance, so that those empty cartons on the lawn would have provided the day's only upset – one minute bump in an otherwise straight, smooth road. He smiled faintly, glad he'd been responsible for that bump. There'd be bigger ones someday, if Brian had his way.

Dale had gone out, in spite of the lateness of the hour, mumbling something about fresh air, and when the film finished at one the family went to bed, leaving the back door unlocked for him. The baby never stirred. Brian slept like a log and woke up at ten with Debbie on his mind.

'Hello?' He stuck a finger in his ear and scowled at the passing truck. 'Is that Mrs Baxter?'

'Yes.' Mrs Baxter had her telephone voice on. 'Who's speaking, please?'

'Brian. Brian Gower. Is Debbie there?'

'Deborah is at home, yes. What do you want?'

'I'd like to speak to her, please. It's important.'

'Ah!' A faint titter. 'I don't imagine you'd have anything really important to say to my daughter, young man. However – just a moment.' A scraping sound as the woman covered the mouthpiece, followed by a muffled 'Deborah – telephone!'

'Stuck-up cow!' he muttered.

'What was that?'

Damn. He'd assumed she wasn't listening. 'Er – stock up now,' he improvised. 'I'm reading an ad in the directory, Mrs Baxter.'

'Hmm. Here's Deborah. Don't keep her chatting all day, will you?' More scraping, then, 'Hello?'

'Hi, Deb. It's me. How you doing?'

'All right, thanks.' Cool. 'What did you say to my mother?'

'Nowt. I was reading her an ad about getting coal in before winter.'

'You're crazy. Did you enjoy the game?'

'Yeah. Look – I want to see you.'

'Why – isn't there a match on anywhere today?'

'Don't be like that, Deb. Can you get out tonight?'

'I could if I wanted to, but I don't know whether I do. I'm not in the mood for a blow-by-blow account of yesterday's game and anyway, what if Royston phones?'

'He won't. And I won't mention football, Deb – promise.'

'Oh, all right.' She had lowered her voice. 'But I'll have to think up a good excuse for Mum. Be in the arcade at seven. I'll get there as soon as I can. OK?'

'Sure. I—'

'What?'

'Nothing. See you around seven then. 'Bye.' He hung up and left the call-box.

4

When he got back from the call-box there was some sort of argument going on between his parents. His father sat staring into his corn-flakes. His hands, curled into fists, lay on the table at either side of his bowl and his cheeks were pale. As Brian walked in his mother was speaking.

'All I'm saying, Ken, is that he shouldn't have done it. That's all. And if he gets in trouble it's his own lookout. He's twenty years old and he ought to have had more sense.' Brian slipped into his place and looked quizzically across at Mick, the only other person present. Mick, apparently anxious not to be involved, merely shrugged and mouthed silently, 'Our Dale.'

'What's our Dale done?' said Brian.

His father shot him a hostile glance. 'Never you mind.'

'He's been and beaten that Pakistani up,' blurted his mother. 'That's what he's done.'

Brian felt himself go cold. 'The landlord – you mean the landlord?' His mother nodded.

'But why?' He turned to his father. 'Why, Dad? He warned our Carole. He didn't want her to have that place. He did his best to put her off.' Close to tears, he leapt up and started towards the door. 'I'm off over there.' He glanced towards the ceiling. 'And I hope that great thick sod up there gets ten years. I hope he gets life!'

He left the house and, half-blind with tears, began stumbling up the road. He hadn't gone twenty metres when he heard footfalls. His father grabbed him by the shoulder and swung him round.

'Listen, Brian!' he hissed. 'I know you're upset, but there's nowt you can do now and if you go shooting your gob off over there, you'll lead the coppers straight to our Dale.'

'Good!' He wrenched himself free. 'I told you – I hope he gets life. I wouldn't be surprised if it was him that did that lass in.'

'Don't say that!' He was seized again, this

time by the sleeve of his jacket. 'Don't ever let me hear you say that again. Our Dale might be a bit violent but he's no killer, Brian. And he's your brother – your own flesh and blood. Nobody turns their own flesh and blood in – nobody. This other feller might be all right – he might be quite a decent bloke but he's a stranger, Brian – a foreigner. Christ knows I'm not prejudiced, but what sort of a bloke'd turn his own brother in for a foreigner, eh? What sort of a bloke?'

Brian's eyes blazed through the tears. 'Brother?' The word choked him. 'I wish he wasn't. I wish I'd never heard of him. He's so thick he can't even get in the army. That guy he beat up's got more brains in his bum than our Dale's got in his head. He wants locking up, our Dale.'

'All right.' His father dropped his hands, freeing him. He spoke quietly. 'You're right. Our Dale's none too bright, I know that. Your mum and I've known since he was six. But won't you just take a minute and think what that means? Put yourself in his shoes. OK?'

Brian shrugged, drawing a sleeve across his eyes to clear them. There was a look in his father's eyes which he'd never seen before – an expression of hurt, a plea, almost. It shocked him, so that his own anger began to dissolve, becoming sadness. He stood with his hands dangling, at a loss. His father was speaking.

'He cares about Carole, right? He doesn't show it, but in his own way he cares about her, and when she shows up scared half to death he wants to help. He wants to do summat for her. Now you and I both know he's got a thing about Pakistanis. Where he got it from I don't know, but lads like our Dale are easily led and I suppose he got talking to the National Front or summat at one time. Anyway, he's got this thing about Pakistanis and our Carole has a room off a Pakistani. You know how he was last week when he found out. Well, it all goes wrong, and so of course Dale says to himself, it's because she got that room off that Pakistani. It's all his fault. I'm off over there and duff him up. He doesn't think, Brian. He follows impulses, that's all. If he goes to jail he'll hardly know why he's there. To him, it will just be another misfortune in a long line of misfortunes and it'll be his mum – your mum – who really gets hurt. D'you understand what I mean?'

Brian nodded, biting his lip. 'I know what you mean, yes. But it doesn't help him, does it? The landlord. He's innocent, Dad. He didn't do anything but he's all smashed up. Did Dale say owt to him – tell him what he was getting it for?'

'Oh aye. This is for my sister. Summat like that, the big daft bugger. Why?'

'Well they're going to come here anyway then, aren't they? They know it was one of

Carole's brothers and it's not hard to guess which. You only have to look at him.'

His father nodded. 'I know. That's what your mum says. But the least we can do is sit tight and keep our mouths shut. He might not go to the police.'

"Course he will. I would. Anyway I won't go. I feel rotten about it but I won't go. Only don't expect me to tell lies for our Dale when the coppers come 'cause I won't. Mum said it's his own lookout and I reckon it is too and I won't lie for him.'

5

The landlord's name is Anwar Patel, and he will not go to the police. Anwar Patel is an illegal immigrant and the less he has to do with the police, the better. In 1966 he surrendered his life savings to a man with a handmade suit and city ways in exchange for a ticket to England. He did not know that what he was doing was illegal, but by the time he had accomplished the journey, in the holds of filthy cargo vessels and on the floors of clapped-out vans, he knew that all was not quite as it ought to be. And shortly after his arrival his exact position was spelled out for him by another man in a handmade suit, who found him a job and then proceeded to extort ten pounds a week from him as the price of silence.

For years, Anwar was unable to save. He ate and slept in one dingy room, with nothing to look forward to but more of the same. The room, too, belonged to the man in the hand-made suit.

Then, one evening in 1977 a different man called on him. A fat man. A prosperous man. A man who smiled a lot, and whose name was Wazir Khan. Wazir Khan owned many shops and he made Anwar manager of one of them.

It was a greengrocery shop, specializing in Indian vegetables, specially imported. The shop did well. As manager, Anwar was decently paid and he didn't have to give up ten pounds a week. The only snag was that Wazir Khan imported other things besides vegetables. Sometimes, Anwar found little packets of white powder hidden among the produce. He was told to keep these little packets somewhere very safe, and from time to time some men came and took them away.

Anwar still manages Wazir's shop. He has no choice. And the little packets still appear, sometimes in the bangun, sometimes among the moolie. Anwar is a landlord, but he is a slave too, and though his lip is cut and his ribs are cracked so that he can scarcely draw breath, he will not go to the police. He knows that if he did, the retribution which would follow would make the blows of the English youth seem like the caress of a pigeon's wing.

6

'Scuse me.' The piping treble cut through the sweaty hubbub of the changing-room. 'Is Brian Gower here?'

'Aye.' Brian stood up, naked to the waist. His knees were caked with mud and blood trickled from a small cut at the corner of his mouth. 'Who wants him?' He peered across the welter of hot, dirty bodies. A first-year kid was hovering in the doorway. Brian beckoned with a jerk of his head and waited while the small boy shoved and wriggled his way across the room.

'What d'you want?'

The kid gulped. He looked, and felt, like a pixie in the middle of a herd of hippos. 'Mr Ramsden sent me. He says would you see him in his room straight after the bell?'

'What for?'

'I don't know. He didn't tell me. He just said to find you and give you the message.'

'So what you waiting for – a tip?'

'N-no.' The small messenger turned and dodged away. Brian followed him with his eyes, feeling like Flashman in *Tom Brown's*

76

Schooldays. His English group was reading *Tom Brown's Schooldays.*

'You wanted to see me, sir?' The mud, and the blood were gone. Brian, pink-faced and freshly combed, stood in the doorway of Ramsden's room.

'Ah yes, Brian. Come in and sit down. It's about this homework.' The master peeled a single sheet from the pile on his desk and scanned it with evident distaste. 'You were asked for a summary of electoral reforms during the nineteenth and twentieth centuries, beginning with the Act of 1832. You were to give the year of each major reform and comment briefly on its effects.'

'Yes, sir.'

'From you, I expected four, five sides – all dates correct and with some intelligent comment. But that was the old you, Brian, not the new you. From the new you I got this single, grubby sheet with, among other bad things, a stultifyingly boring assessment of the effects of the Act of 1942: an Act which does not exist. What's the matter, Brian, eh? What's happening to you, lad?'

Brian stared down at his clasped hands, feeling his cheeks redden. He knew the piece wasn't up to scratch; knew nothing had been up to scratch lately. He knew why, too. What he didn't know was whether Ramsden was genuinely interested in the reasons, or whether this interview was just a bollocking to gee him up a bit. He decided to try the truth.

'I – did it in my bedroom. Our Dale was there, playing records. I asked him to stop but he wouldn't. We don't get on, sir.'

The master tilted his head with a faint smile and murmured, 'That does not surprise me.' Dale had passed through school and Ramsden remembered him. 'But could you not work in another part of the house?'

'There's nowhere, sir. My sister's got the other bedroom. Her kid witters all the time with his teeth. The telly's on downstairs and my mum's in and out of the kitchen, clattering things. I can't concentrate, sir.'

'No.' Ramsden stared out of the window. Brian waited, wishing he had the guts to get up and leave. After a minute the master looked at him and said, 'I happen to think you've got something, Brian. Something worth cultivating. Until just recently your work has been of a consistently high standard, and that includes your homework. I believe you have it in you to succeed, and it would be a pity if you were to let your chances slip because of minor irritations at home.'

Minor irritations. Brian caught his bottom lip between his teeth. He wanted to shout out that the things he'd been talking about were not minor irritations. That continual noise has a way of numbing the brain, so that it isn't so much a matter of letting your chances slip as of having them ripped from your grasp. He wanted to explain that the effects were cumulative – that just because you managed to turn in decent homework for two years didn't mean you could go on doing it for four or five. That eventually you knew you weren't going to beat them, and that at that point the urge to join them became overwhelming.

Suddenly, for no apparent reason, Barry Weatherall came into his head and he found himself wondering how he might handle a confrontation like this one. He wouldn't start crying and pour out his troubles, which was what Brian felt like doing. Neither would he apologize and mumble some sort of half-promise about trying to do better, as a way of bringing the interview to a close. He'd probably have got up and left while Ramsden was looking out of the window. If he'd bothered to turn up in the first place, which Brian doubted.

I'm not Barry Weatherall, he told himself. But I'm not an anorak either, and I'm through being the soft one of the family. He lifted his head. 'You don't know anything about me,' he said.

For a second, Ramsden looked startled. Then his features hardened. 'I'm sorry you've chosen to take this attitude,' he said crisply. 'I asked you to come and see me because I wanted to help you. I thought you'd respond in a positive way but it seems I was wrong. You've got potential, Brian, there's no doubt about that, but if you choose to waste it there's nothing I or anybody else can do about it. I only wish I could be sure you understand what you're doing.'

'Can I go now?' He had to force himself to say the words. His instinct was to capitulate: to react as he always had in such situations, but he had set a course for himself and for once he was going to stick to it.

Ramsden sighed. 'Yes, Brian. You may go. You know where I am if you change your mind.'

When he got outside everybody else had gone. He swung his battered bag over his shoulder and started to walk slowly up through the estate while a confusion of thoughts and feelings chased one another across his mind. A part of him was glad – elated even – that he had taken the line he had with Ramsden. What he had told the master was undoubtedly true – that he knew nothing about the lives of those he taught. How could he? He was posh: a Duchy Drive type with plenty of brass and an ordered life. On the other hand he was a decent feller. The sort who'd talk to you as if you were a human being and even have the occasional laugh. So, while one part of Brian fiercely rejoiced, misgivings lurked elsewhere. What boats had he burned? Was there a way back, and if so would he ever want to take it? The stone he had thrown in Bournemouth, and the words he had spoken just now to Ramsden had killed off the old Brian Gower, but who was he now? He was no Barry Weatherall and he was no anorak either. He wasn't a rebel and he wasn't a swot. Easy to say what he was not, but what the heck was he?

'I'm me,' he told himself. 'Me. No-one knows me and no-one owns me. I'm me, that's all, and I go my own way from now on.'

It was a lonely feeling.

7

Brian looked at his watch. Another five minutes and the bouncers'd be round, urging the kids to finish their Cokes and leave.

It was ten to nine, and at Giggles the Friday night Young Teens session was drawing to a close. The DJ had faded-in the final record. The bar staff flitted to and fro, clearing cans and glasses in preparation for the influx of adults at nine. A few older people were already in. They stood about in groups or leant against the bar with their hands in their pockets, watching the kids: waiting for them to vacate their seats so they could grab the best tables.

Debbie was slurping up the dregs of her Coke through a pink and white straw. Brian watched how the lights turned her hair green, then blue, then pink. A bouncer loomed.

'Come on, son, let's have that glass.' Brian threw back his head and drained his glass, leaving two bits of ice clinking in the bottom. He thrust it towards the bouncer. 'Bourbon,' he drawled. 'On the rocks.'

'Got your birth certificate, have you?'

'No. They weren't invented when I was born.'

'Like hell.' The man glanced at Debbie. 'Come on, love.'

The tip of Debbie's straw described a sputtering circle round the bottom of her glass. She handed him the empty and he moved on. They were about to get up when a figure emerged from the gloom and dealt Brian a mighty slap between the shoulder-blades.

'Hiya, kid. Smashed any good cars up lately?' The force of the blow rocked Brian forward in his chair. He twisted round. Barry Weatherall grinned down at him.

'No.' He forced a smile, trying not to show that the slap had hurt and startled him. 'Not lately. Might do a few tonight though.'

Weatherall laughed. 'Not on Coke you won't. How about having a real drink with me and my mates?' He nodded to where four or five of the Ointment were waiting by the bar. Brian pulled a face.

'Can't. I'm only fifteen.'

'So who's to know in this light? There's always a few kids stay. No-one's bothered.'

'We are,' said Debbie. Weatherall looked at her.

'Why? You look older than he does. You'd pass for eighteen easy.'

'We don't want to.' She looked at Brian. 'What's he on about, smashing cars up?' Brian had thought it wise not to tell her about the Bournemouth incident.

'Oh,' he said, airily. 'There was a spot of bother after the Bournemouth game. I smashed a car window.'

'You did? How come you didn't tell me?'

'I don't tell you everything.' It was an uncharacteristic response, but the sort of thing Brian imagined the Ointment might approve of.

Debbie stood up, furious. 'OK. If that's the way it is, I'm off. And don't think you can call me tomorrow and make it all right, 'cause you can't.' She snatched up her handbag and made for the exit, wobbling a little on her high heels.

Brian gazed after her, feeling his heart sink. He was about to forfeit his new macho image by running after her when the older boy patted him on the shoulder. 'That's the way to handle 'em,' he growled. 'Rule your floggin' life if you give 'em half a chance. What you having?'

Brian watched Debbie disappear through the swing doors. 'What?'

'I said what you having – to drink, dummy!'

'Oh! Bourbon I guess. Or martini.'

'Bourbon?' exploded Weatherall. 'Mar-cowing-tini?' Heads turned, seeking the cause of the big lad's mirth. Brian flushed, looking at his hands on the table. 'What d'you think you're on – *Cheers*? You'll have a pint of bitter, same as the rest of us. OK?'

Brian nodded. Anything to shut the great loobie up before a bouncer came to see what all the fuss was about.

8

Debbie paused under the awning and inhaled deeply. There was a sharpness in the air tonight: the tang of approaching autumn. It cleared her head and she was able to think objectively about what had occurred inside.

He'd been showing off. Lads did it all the time. Acting tough. If she waited a minute or so, here under the pink and green neon, he'd come hurrying after her, full of clumsy contri-tion. Brian wasn't tough. He was one of the gentlest lads she'd ever known. It was one of the things she liked about him. He was going through some sort of phase, that's all.

Courting notoriety. Seeking the approval of pillocks like Aziz and Weatherall. He'd be getting up now, mumbling excuses and heading for the door. Blushing, probably. When he appeared, she'd act cool. Let him dangle for a while. Make him feel bad.

She glanced both ways along the street. The kids had dispersed. An older couple brushed past her, going in. A brief burst of music and a waft of warm air. A car slowed, winking, and turned into the car-park. A door slammed. A figure approached. A man by himself, dangling keys. Something familiar about him. He entered the neon glow and smiled at her and she recognized Royston Ambler.

'Hello, love. Deserted you, has he?'

'N-no.' Flushing. Shaking her head. 'He's coming. He went to the gents.'

'I'll wait with you till he comes, then. All right?'

'No.' She was confused. He was older. Seemed to know she was lying. She couldn't cope with him.

'Why not; where's the harm?'

'He's not coming. We had a fight. I was just leaving.'

Ambler nodded. 'I thought it was something like that.' He grinned. 'Look – why don't I run you home in the car. It'll only take five minutes and it'll save you a fair walk.'

'No thanks.' She fancied it, though. Brian

would go apeshape when he found out. Serve him right.

'Oh, come on. I'd like to drive you.'

'No. You were just going in. I don't want to—'

'It's no trouble, really.'

She shook her head, wishing Brian would come; knowing he wouldn't now. 'No. I'll walk. It's hot in there and the fresh air'll do me good. Thanks anyway.' She started to walk away. He called after her.

'Take care, then. I'll see you around.'

'See you.' She felt she'd been ungrateful. Maybe she should've let him drive her after all. Too late now. She walked on.

9

'Here, get that off and get stuck into this.' The blond-haired youth shoved the half-empty glass into Brian's hands and plonked down a full one. Brian forced himself to take a long pull, holding his breath so as not to taste it. He felt sick. The music seemed to have got a lot louder and he couldn't focus on things. He felt unreal, sitting here among the heavies and the birds they'd pulled. For a time he'd lapped it up, swigging and swapping wisecracks. Everybody seemed to have forgotten the bourbon incident and he'd almost managed to convince himself he was one of them.

Now he'd had enough. More than enough. The place was hot and smoky and he had just enough wit left to know that the girls kept making crude cracks about him – about his youth, his inexperience and the probable size of certain bits of his anatomy – which the Ointment seemed to find hugely funny.

One of the girls – Wendy or Wanda or some such name – had an enormous mouth full of dirty, greenish teeth with bits of peanut lodged between them. When she laughed, which was often, Brian found himself gazing into this mouth and imagining what it would be like to have a really good snogging session with Wendy. Every time he thought about this a wave of nausea hit him, but for some reason he could neither stop thinking about it nor tear his eyes away from that horrible mouth. He realized dimly that he was drunk, and that these people were trying to make a prannock out of him.

He was halfway down his fourth pint – or was it his fifth? – when he spotted Royston Ambler standing at the bar. To his fuddled mind, this seemed like a godsend. Now he'd show 'em. Now they'd see what sort of a guy he really was. Nobody makes a prannock out of Brian Gower. He pawed at Weatherall's sleeve.

'Hey, Barry – see that guy over there – him with the poncy jacket?'

Weatherall nodded. 'What about him?'

'He keeps pestering my bird. He's nineteen, and I'm off over there to smash his face in.'

Weatherall gazed speculatively across at Brian's intended victim. 'He'll have you for breakfast, kid.'

'He bloody won't!' Brian lurched to his feet, knocking over his pint.

'Hey, watch it!' Wendy leapt back in her seat to dodge the spillage. Weatherall grabbed Brian's wrist. 'Siddown, you daft little dork – you're pissed.'

'I'm not!' He jerked himself free. 'I'm gonna get him.' He turned. Anger, and the need to redeem himself in the eyes of the Ointment had swamped his nausea, but he was unsteady on his feet and everything outside his direct line of vision was a blur. He seemed to be walking very slowly along a roaring tunnel with Royston Ambler under spotlights at the end.

'Ambler!' His cry was unpremeditated. It surprised him, as though somebody else had uttered it. The youth either didn't hear, or chose to ignore him. Somewhere, somebody laughed.

'Ambler!' This time he turned his head. Brian saw the surprise on his face. 'I'm gonna smash your face in, Ambler.' He had difficulty getting his tongue round the words and the carpet seemed to undulate as he advanced.

Ambler set down his half of lager and

straightened up, watching him. Brian saw a glint of malicious amusement in his eyes. Somebody said something, and several people laughed. Brian didn't care. They were nothing: bits of tunnel-wall. Only Ambler mattered. And the Ointment at his back, watching.

The gap between them shrank. Ambler's mouth moved. The words seemed to come from a great way off. 'Go home, kiddo. Nobody wants to fight you. Go before you get hurt.'

'It's you who's gonna get hurt!' Brian flung himself at the youth. Ambler sidestepped and pushed a hand into his face. It wasn't a punch. It wasn't even a slap, but it was enough to knock Brian off balance. He ran forward in a sort of dive, clutching at the garments of strangers, and crashed full-length on the carpet, catching his cheek on the brass foot-rail.

He was not down long. Rough hands seized him and hauled him to his feet. Somebody grabbed his collar and the seat of his pants and he was running – running involuntarily with his pants cutting into his crotch and his feet almost clear of the floor. Everybody was laughing. The open doorway loomed. He tried to grab the doorposts, but he missed. There was cold air and a blur of neon and then the grip on his pants and collar was gone and he went sprawling.

This time, nobody picked him up. He lay face-down on the pavement with the taste of blood in his mouth. Nothing hurt, but there was a roaring in his ears and when he closed his eyes the rotation of the earth threatened to hurl him off into the void. He spread his fingers on the cold flags and held on.

Presently, the chill that struck through his clothing and seeped into his bones sobered him a little, and he became aware that he was in danger. It only needed a policeman to come along and find him like this and he'd be up before the beak. Drunk and incapable. He could just see it in the *Telegraph*. Brian Gower, aged fifteen, drunk and incapable in Darley Street. Mum'd love that. Debbie's mum would love it even more and it'd be a big hit at school, too. He pictured old Dodgson opening his paper and learning that one of his fifth formers had been found on the pavement outside Giggles, pissed out of his skull. He was always on about the good name of the school, was Dodgson. Maybe he'd put Brian's name on the honours board: B. Gower – BA (Hons) – Drunkenness.

He giggled, and began tackling the business of getting to his feet. It wasn't easy. As soon as he lifted his head everything spun. He paused on hands and knees, shaking his head in a useless bid to stop the giddying rotation. A part of him longed to lie down and go to sleep but when he let his eyes close the spinning got

90

worse and he nearly threw up. He tried taking some deep breaths, and presently he was able to crawl to the nearest lamp post and use it to drag himself upright.

As soon as he was on his feet the nausea returned and he bent forward, one arm wrapped round the lamp post, and vomited into the gutter. He was vaguely aware that somebody was passing by. A middle-aged couple. The man muttered something that sounded condemnatory and the woman responded with a lot of tutting. Brian wanted to turn round and tell them to piss off, but he was feeling too wretched to bother and the moment passed.

He didn't know how long he stood there, waiting for some improvement in his condition. Cars went by, and people, and he got very cold. After what seemed a very long time he felt sufficiently steady on his feet to leave his friend the lamp post and begin making his way home. There were plenty of people about, but nobody took any notice of him. In fact they seemed to shun him: swerving to leave him plenty of room and avoiding him also with their eyes, as though he was one of the Venn Street drunks.

He thought about Debbie: her angry face and the way she'd wobbled off across the floor, and a wave of sadness engulfed him. He began to cry quietly as he walked. He wished she was here now, so he could tell her he didn't mean whatever it was he'd said to offend her. He couldn't remember exactly what he'd said, but he knew it had amounted to choosing the company of the Ointment over hers. He'd hurt her; lost her, probably for their sake, and all they'd done was make a pillock out of him and get him like this and then laugh when he got thrown out.

He wished he could go back in time – back to nine o'clock. He'd choose to leave with Deb this time, and the Ointment could think what they liked. They wouldn't get the chance to make a fool of him, and he wouldn't be there to make a fool of himself with that Ambler prannock. Aye, he told himself bitterly. Wouldn't that be great, eh? To go back in time, knowing what I know now, and to do everything right. It was probably the same with the Venn Street drunks. There'd be a time – a moment long ago in each of their lives, when if they'd acted differently they'd have gone on being ordinary people. He wondered if they ever thought about that. It would hurt to think about it, because you can't ever go back. Maybe they drank so they didn't have to think about it. So that they couldn't. He wondered whether tonight was a turning point in his own life, and he shivered.

10

'Is something the matter, love? You look as though you've been crying.'

Debbie shook her head. 'I haven't. I had something in my eye but it's gone now.' She hung up her coat and followed her mother into the living-room. Her mother had been standing at the open front door when Debbie had turned the corner. Getting a bit of fresh air, she said. Debbie had her doubts.

Her father was watching TV. He glanced up, smiling. 'Where's my favourite girl been this evening, eh?'

'Giggles.' No point telling more lies than necessary. He shook his head. 'I wish you wouldn't, Deb. You know how your mother and I feel about places like that.'

'I know, Dad, but all the kids go. I wouldn't have any friends if I never went to wine-bars.'

'And which particular friend were you with tonight?' Her mother managed to make the word friend sound sinister. 'The Gower boy, I suppose?'

'No.' Debbie sat down on the sofa. If she'd said yes, she'd have set herself up for a major interrogation. She didn't need it. Not tonight. 'I went with Leanne. We drank Coke and danced a bit. With each other.'

'What – no boys?' Her mother sounded

sceptical. Debbie decided to try a slice of the truth.

'Yes, there was one. Royston Ambler. We talked. He offered to run me home.'

Her father raised his eyebrows. 'The lad who helped you with your bags at Sainsbury's – Seth Ambler's lad?'

Debbie nodded.

'But he must be eighteen or nineteen by now. What's he want to bother with a lass of your age for?'

Debbie shrugged. 'I dunno. He seems to like me. He asked me to go out with him that time at the supermarket.'

'And have you been out with him?'

She shook her head. 'No, Dad, of course I haven't. He's nineteen. You'd go mad if I said I'd been out with him, wouldn't you?'

To her surprise, her father looked uncertain. 'I don't know, Deb. He's a decent sort of lad, and his father's one of the most highly respected men in Barfax. It's a pity he's so much older than you, that's all.'

'You could do a lot worse, Deborah,' said her mother, adding with a smirk, 'you've been doing a lot worse.'

Debbie bit her lip and looked at the floor. Before tonight, her mother's remark would have been enough to send her storming off to her room in a barrage of door-slamming. Now she only said, 'You needn't worry. It's over between me and Brian.' Saying the words started her crying again. She got up and hurried from the room, holding a tissue over her nose and mouth.

Behind her, her parents exchanged glances. Her father's expression was one of perplexity and concern. He would have got up and gone after his daughter, but his wife placed a hand on his arm.

'Let her go, Len.' She spoke softly, but he saw the triumph in her eyes. 'She's young. She'll get over it in no time, you'll see.'

11

Brian woke up feeling vile. His brain had been replaced by a sliding brick which crashed into the walls of his skull every time he moved his head. His throat felt raw and his stomach muscles ached from vomiting. When he tried opening his eyes they were lanced with needles of steely light.

'Aaagh,' he groaned. Instead of a tongue, there was a dead mole in his mouth. 'Bleaugh.'

Above him and a little to the left, somebody chuckled. Brian opened one eye. Mick grinned down at him. 'How you feeling, kid?'

Brian winced by way of an answer.

'By gum – you had a skinful last night, didn't you? I thought it was all Coke and stuff down Giggles?'

'I – stayed on. Barry Weatherall. Did Mum and Dad notice owt?'

'No. You came in and staggered straight upstairs. I could tell, but they had summat more important to think about.'

'Like what?'

'Like the factory's closing and Dad's redundant, that's what.'

'Huh?' He jerked his head off the pillow and the brick slammed into the back of his skull. He sank back, aware of a raging thirst. 'You're having me on, aren't you?'

'Wish I was. They finish two weeks yesterday. Great, eh?'

'Great.' He lay absolutely still with eyes closed. The mole in his mouth wasn't dead after all, because it kept crapping. He could taste it. He remembered how Debbie had flounced out on him, and how Ambler had sent him flying. The bum's rush through the door and Barry Weatherall's silly laugh.

'Hey Mick,' he croaked. 'If I don't drink owt, how long will it be before I'm dead?'

12

He'd probably have stayed in bed all day if it hadn't been for his paper round. As it was, he had to get up at seven and stagger round the quiet streets. He was home by eight, gagging for a drink. Everybody else was up by then. Dad and Dale were outside, messing about with the car. Mick had just left for the Chicken Shack and Carole was watching cartoons on TV with little Nick on her knee. Mum was in the kitchen. She looked at him when he walked in.

'You look a bit green round the gills,' she said. 'What were you up to last night?'

He shook his head, filling a cup at the cold tap and trying not to look at the nappy in the sink. 'Nowt much. I had seventeen pints in the Unicorn, smoked forty fags, shot some smack in the bus-shelter and had fish and chips on the way home. And all for under a quid and all.'

'Don't talk so daft, our Brian. And don't think I don't know what smack is, neither. You'd better not let your dad hear you so much as mention the stuff, or it'll be another sort of smack you'll get, lad. You're not too big, y'know.'

'Aye, I know.' He drank greedily and refilled the cup. 'D'you know where my scarf and cap are, Mum? It's Wigan this aft, at home.'

'They'll be where you left them. I've better things to do than trail round after you, picking stuff up. Did you get paid?'

''Course.'

'Then I'll have the fiver you borrowed. And try to make your money last a week from now on. Your dad's lost his job and I won't have owt to lend.'

'I know. Our Mick told me. I always knew Ambler was a pillock. His lad is, and all.'

'I wouldn't know. D'you want some breakfast?'

'Ugh! No thanks.' He drained the cup a second time and put it upside down on the drainer.

'Have you finished at the sink?' asked Carole, peering round the kitchen door. 'Can I get my nappy now?'

'Aye.' Brian stepped aside. 'Only I thought it was the baby's.'

The afternoon was drizzly with a blustery wind, but there was a good crowd at Hillside. Brian stood with his shoulders hunched and his hands in his jacket pockets, gazing across the muddy pitch. The clock under the balcony at the far end showed ten to three.

'How d'you think we'll do then, Colin?'

'Murder 'em, man.'

The Ointment thought so too, if their chanting was anything to go by.

'Dickie Lester's Barfax Army, We're not daft, we're friggin' barmy—'

'You are and all,' growled Brian sourly. He'd wandered down the Arndale in the middle of the morning hoping to see Debbie, but she hadn't shown up. He'd had to force himself not to phone her. He was full of futile regret and the Ointment were by no means his favourite people.

The Wigan players appeared and began warming up. A couple of minutes later Town ran out to loud cheering, with the officials trotting in their wake. Wigan won the toss and made the goalkeepers change ends.

'Bad omen, that,' said Jonathan.

'Rubbish!' retorted Colin, and Lee yelled, 'Come on, Town!'

The first half was a dull affair. Both sides had begun the season well, and seemed reluctant to take the sort of risks that might jeopardize their positions near the top of the league. There was a lot of midfield stuff, too many offside traps and too much passing back. It was an attempted pass back by the unfortunate Rickstraw that let Wigan in just before half-time. He intercepted the ball just outside his own penalty area and, finding himself hemmed in by Wigan players, turned and, without really looking, punted the ball back towards his goalie. MacNee was off his line, having come out in anticipation of a shot from the man Rickstraw had robbed. The surface was greasy, the pass inaccurate, and the stunned Town fans watched in horror as the ball, deflected slightly by the outstretched fingers of the fallen goalie, trickled over the line. Seconds later the whistle brought the half to a close and the dejected Barfax squad trooped off to the jeers of both sets of supporters.

'Rickstraw,' snarled Colin, gazing after the unlucky player, 'you're a wassock. A chunky, hand-crafted, twenty-two carat wassock.'

'They all are,' said Brian. 'I wouldn't give you fifty pence for the lot of 'em. That prat Ambler should've shut this lot down and kept the factory open.'

'Yeah. My old man and my mum are both out of work now. Maybe they'll come and play for the Town. Couldn't do no worse than this lot, anyway.'

'Anybody want a pie or owt?' asked Jonathan. 'I'm off for one.'

'I don't want a pie,' Jeannette told him, 'I want a pee. Why is it that there's a gents at the back of the Kop, but no ladies?'

'Ladies don't stand on the Kop,' grinned Jonathan. Jeannette thumped him on the arm.

In their half of the Kop, the Wigan fans were celebrating their team's lead: holding their scarves aloft and swaying. The Ointment retaliated with a threat: *You're gonna get your friggin' heads kicked in—'*

'They won't, though,' said Jeannette. 'Not now. Have you noticed?' She nodded towards the floodlight pylon at the end of the terrace. TV cameras had been clamped on to its steel legs at various heights and angles, so that they covered the whole of the Kop.

'Bloody hell!' cried Colin. 'When did they put them up? Big Brother is watching you. I wonder if they can see into the bog?'

'If they can, you'll get nicked for carrying an offensive weapon,' Lee told him.

'Where's the screens?' asked Brian. 'In t'police station or what?'

'No, thickhead. They're in that van over there.' Jeannette pointed towards the Director's Box, where a vehicle stood in the shadows under the balcony. 'It's a hoolivan. Didn't you see the bit in the *Telegraph* about it? It's got a row of screens and a snatch-squad. If they see owt on t'screen – bother starting or summat – they pile out and grab the leaders.'

Colin shook his head. 'We don't get the *Telegraph*. I saw the van, but I thought it was the St John's.'

'They want to start by snatching Ambler,' growled Brian.

'Yeah!' Jonathan grinned through a mouthful of Cornish pasty. 'March him out with his arm up his back.' The others laughed.

'No, I mean it,' insisted Brian. 'If the Ointment had broken into the lamp factory and smashed it up so it had to close down,

101

they'd have got about ten years, and people'd have gone on about what bastards they were, putting everybody out of work. Well – that's exactly what Ambler's done, right? Why should he get off scot-free where the Ointment wouldn't – what's the difference?'

'It's his factory,' said Jonathan, through another mouthful. 'I mean, you can do what you want with your own stuff, can't you?'

'Aye, but that doesn't make it right though, does it? Not when it puts hundreds of people on t'benefit. There ought to be a law that you can't throw folk out of work.'

'Well there won't be,' put in Jeannette, 'so you might as well belt up. Anyway, here come the lads.'

For the next forty-five minutes Town threw everything forward, but they failed to crack Wigan's defence. When the final whistle blew it was still one–nil to the visitors, and it was a dejected crowd that streamed out through the gates. By the time the next home match was played, many of them would be on the dole and eight pounds fifty would be hard to find. Gates would fall and this would affect the team's morale, so that far from pressing for promotion, the Town side might find itself in a desperate fight to keep from going down.

PART THREE

GOING DOWN

1

In the middle of October, the school Drama Society started rehearsing its Christmas play. This year it was *King Lear*. The big parts went to members of the Society, but as usual there weren't enough members to fill all the bit-parts and take care of scene-shifting and other menial tasks, and a notice appeared on the bulletin-board asking for volunteers.

Debbie was a member of the Society. She wasn't a bad actress, and had landed a couple of plum roles in past productions. This time she'd be playing Cordelia.

Brian saw the notice one breaktime when he was loitering to avoid having to go outside. It was a raw, wet day and he was pretending to read the team lists, posters, and announcements pinned to the board when Ryder hove in view. Ryder was a sixth former, a prefect, and a spack. He'd never liked Brian, and now that his enemy seemed to have suffered a fall from grace, he missed no opportunity to hassle him.

'Come on, Gower – outside. You know the rule.'

'I'm reading. Anyway it's pissing down.'

'Makes no difference. A rule's a rule. Everybody else is out.'

'More fool them. Anyway, I've got to see Ramsden.'

'What about?'

'This.' Brian nodded at the notice. 'They want scene-shifters and Ramsden's stage-manager.' He'd only just spotted the notice and had no intention of volunteering, but he was damned if he was going to let Ryder send him out. The prefect peered at the notice.

'You can see him after school, can't you?'

'No. See this?' Brian tapped the word 'urgently' which had been typed in capitals and underlined. 'Urgently, Ryder. Urgently required. That means—'

'I know what urgently means.'

'Well then.'

'All right.' The prefect's tone was a blend of anger and resignation. 'Go see him, but don't let me catch you loitering about after, that's all.'

'You're a great guy, Ryder. I always said so.'

Brian made his way towards the staff-room. He meant to pass by and hang about the corridors and changing-rooms till end of break, but as he walked it struck him that it might not be a bad idea to volunteer, at that. For one thing, Debbie was in the Drama Society. Since the Giggles incident she'd steadfastly refused to have anything to do with him, but if they had to stay behind for rehearsals and things, maybe he'd get the chance to talk to her. He didn't like admitting it, even to himself, but he'd been missing her badly.

And then there was Ramsden. They'd got on well at one time, but since that stupid interview Brian had noted a sharp cooling-off in the master's attitude towards him. It wasn't surprising of course, but it seemed to have spread. He'd had good relationships with a number of his teachers but these too had deteriorated lately, and he sensed that they now lumped him in with the unco-operative element in the school. He didn't exactly regret what he'd said to Ramsden – it was the truth after all – but now, with GCSE year well under way, he felt it might be a good idea to ease the situation a bit, and volunteering to help with the play might be a good way to start.

He knocked on the staff-room door. It was opened by Miss Carmody. She was six feet tall and taught biology.

'Yes.'

'Is Mr Ramsden in, please?'

'He is.' She made no move to get Ramsden, but stood looking down at him through her gold-rimmed spectacles as though he were a specimen of faeces.

'Can I have a word with him, please?'

'No doubt you can, since you possess a perfectly good set of vocal chords. Whether you may or not is another matter. Wait.' She pushed the door to. After a moment Ramsden opened it.

'Well, Gower – what d'you want?'

'I – saw the notice, sir.'

'Notice?'

'Yessir. About the play. I've come to volunteer as a scene-shifter.'

'Hmm. Well, Gower, I'm not sure we can use you. We need reliable people, you see – people who'll turn up regularly. Punctual people. People who aren't afraid of hard work, and I'm not sure you fit into that category nowadays, lad. D'you know what I mean?'

Brian felt a surge of anger. The pillock hadn't forgotten then. He'd been harbouring a grudge and now he was working it off.

'I'm reliable, sir.' He wanted to add that you don't need a quiet place to shift scenery, but decided against it. He was here to mend fences, not tear them down.

'Are you now?' The man regarded him in silence. Brian looked down, shifting his weight from foot to foot, wishing he hadn't come. After a while Ramsden said, 'If you give up your crown, Gower, you needn't expect people to go on treating you as a king.'

Brian looked at him, frowning. 'Crown, sir?'

'Yes, Gower. Crown. D'you know the play?'

'What play, sir?'

'*Lear*, lad. The one you're volunteering to help with.'

'No, sir. I didn't think I'd need to, just to hump scenery about.'

Ramsden smiled briefly. 'Read it. Not because you're going to shift scenery, but because you're a bit of a Lear yourself. Come to the drama hall on Thursday at four. We'll be painting flats.'

Ramsden went in and closed the door. Brian stood for a moment, looking at it. Crown. Flats. What the heck was the wassock on about? Anyway, it seemed he was hired. Thursday at four. He was heading for the changing-rooms and keeping an eye open for Ryder when the buzzer went for the end of break.

2

As it turned out, Brian's scene-shifting didn't bring him into contact with Debbie much at all. Rehearsals took place at odd times and in various parts of the school, often with nothing but tables and chairs for props, and Ramsden's team was not involved. Their sessions were after school, when they gathered in the store-room in the back of the drama hall to knock up bits of scenery and paint them. Nevertheless, Brian found the work interesting and after a week or two he thought he detected a slight thaw in the staff's attitude towards him.

His big reward came on the afternoon of bonfire night. The school always had its own bonfire, with a fireworks display paid for out of PTA funds and organized by staff members and a few parents.

The drama store was cluttered with a decade's accumulation of old, broken furniture and torn flats, and Ramsden decided that bonfire night would be a good time to get rid of it all. As always, the fire was built straight after school on the fifth, and a lot of pupils hung about to watch. When Ramsden's team emerged, staggering from the drama hall with their burdens, some of the smaller kids cheered, and when a second load followed, and then a third, they clutched one another's sleeves and gasped. The stack was five metres high and growing. It was going to be the biggest fire the school had ever had, and easily the biggest in Barfax.

Brian was sweating like a pig. He had just stacked his third load and was wiping his brow with his sleeve when he spotted Debbie among the spectators. He caught her eyes and grinned, and to his surprise she smiled back. He went across to her and said, 'Some fire, huh?'

She nodded. 'What're you doing anyway,

110

humping stuff around? You're usually fifty miles away when there's anything strenuous to be done.'

'Ah well – I'm one of Ramsden's team for the play, aren't I? Scene-shifting.'

'Really? I didn't know. I'm Cordelia.'

'I know.' He decided to wade right in. 'That's why I volunteered.'

She looked at him. 'You mean you're only helping because I'm in the play?'

'Aye. I thought it might – get us back together, like.'

'Oh.' She said nothing more and her eyes avoided his. After a while he said, 'Are you coming to the fire?'

'Yes.'

'Who with?'

'Leanne.'

'How about coming with me?'

'What about Leanne?'

'She could come with us.'

'OK. Where shall we see you?'

'I'll be at the end of your road at half seven. All right?'

'All right.'

When Debbie turned the corner at twenty-five to eight, she was alone.

'Where's Leanne?'

She shrugged. 'I dunno. She was supposed to call for me at quarter past seven.'

'Did she know I was coming?'

'No. We fixed it this afternoon, before I knew.'

'I wondered if I'd put her off.'

'No. Someone else might have asked her – one of the lads. But I'd have thought she'd phone or something.'

'Why? You didn't phone her about me.'

'No, but I wasn't breaking my arrangement with her, was I? Anyway, we'll probably see her there. Come on.'

They lingered a bit on the way, making up for their separation, and the stack was already ablaze when they reached the playing field. It was a cold, misty evening but dry, and the flames illuminated several hundred faces. Practically the whole school was there, and a lot of the younger kids had brought their parents with them. There were some ex-pupils too, and a few people from round about. Debbie and Brian threaded their way to the front and stood with their arms round each other's waists, enjoying their reconciliation and the heat on their faces.

Debbie's eyes searched the crowd. 'I don't see Leanne.'

Brian shook his head. 'You'd be lucky to spot her in this lot. She'll be here somewhere.'

At nine o'clock the fireworks began. Everybody stood with their backs to the fire and oo'd and ah'd as one gorgeous display followed another. Brian hadn't bought fireworks himself for two or three years but he knew how expensive they were, and he marvelled at the thought that these people, many of them out of work and on their uppers, must be watching at least a thousand quid go up in smoke. It was a breathtakingly beautiful spectacle and you've got to have a bit of fun sometimes, but he couldn't help feeling there was something cock-eyed somewhere.

After the fireworks there were jacket potatoes, parkin pigs and toffee. The fire had become a mound of incandescent ash which glowed and rippled with the wind like something breathing. The adults and older pupils gathered round it, eating and chatting while the smaller kids chased one another about in the outer darkness, squealing and laughing.

At half-past ten it began to drizzle. By this time most of the small children had been dragged away to bed, and now the rest of the crowd began to disperse, hunching into coat collars and calling their goodnights. By eleven only a handful remained, and these were mainly couples like Debbie and Brian. They stood, leaning into one another, watching two teachers tidying up with rakes: scraping scattered fragments of combustible material into the shrinking ash pile.

'I think we'd better go,' whispered Debbie. 'I'm getting soaked and my mum'll be getting suspicious.'

They walked slowly through the nearly

empty streets, not wanting the evening to end. Hours of gazing into the fire had left luminous blobs floating in front of their eyes. They talked softly and held on to each other, walking in step.

As they approached the corner where they'd have to say goodnight, they saw a knot of people standing under a street lamp, watching their progress. With a sharp intake of breath, Debbie snatched her arm away and twisted free of Brian's. He looked at her.

'What's up?'

'Sssh! It's my mum and dad. I think you'd better go, Brian. Go on.'

'No, I'm not going. We haven't done anything wrong.'

'Debbie?' Her father started towards them, calling her name.

She shoved Brian away from her. 'Go, Brian, please – I don't want you getting any hassle from him. Go, quick.'

Brian shook his head, watching the man, who didn't even glance at him but grabbed his daughter by the shoulders and snapped, 'Where's Leanne?'

Debbie shook her head. 'We haven't seen her. Why?'

'Was she at the fire?'

'We don't know, Mr Baxter,' said Brian. 'What's up?'

The others were approaching. There were

three of them. Leanne's parents, guessed Brian. And of course Debbie's mum. Ignoring his question, Baxter dropped his hands and turned to them.

'They haven't seen her. I'm sorry. I think we'd better call the police.'

The woman let out an odd, muted cry and the man reached for her, holding her to him; patting her on the back as if she were a baby. Debbie, wild-eyed now, looked at her father.

'Dad – what's the matter?' Her voice rose on a wave of dread. 'Why won't you tell me what's wrong?'

Baxter cast a glance in the direction of the weeping woman and spoke quietly. 'Leanne set off at seven, saying she was coming to our house. As you know, she never arrived. When she wasn't home by eleven, the Stantons got worried and phoned to ask if you were in yet. I said you weren't, and that Leanne hadn't been here at all, so then Mr Stanton phoned another friend of Leanne's to see if she'd been there, and she told him she saw Leanne getting into a car in Foston Lane just after seven.'

3

When Brian got home he found that his mother had just beaten him to it. She was hanging her coat up. She'd taken a part-time job cleaning at the hospital and they didn't finish till half-past ten.

'Phew!' She wafted the air with her hand and moved aside to let Brian hang his jacket up. 'You stink of smoke, lad. I'll have to wash everything you've got on.'

'I know. It was a smoky fire. Leanne Stanton's disappeared.'

'What?' They went down the hall and into the front room. The table was set and a frying smell drifted in from the kitchen. Carole was watching TV.

'I said Leanne Stanton's missing. Somebody saw her getting into a car at seven o'clock and she's not been seen since.'

'Oh heck.' His mother's brow puckered with concern. 'She hasn't got a boyfriend with a car, has she?'

Brian shook his head. 'She hasn't a boyfriend at all that I know of.'

'Oh dear. How did you hear about it?'

'I was walking Debbie home.'

He told her what had happened. 'They went in to phone the police. Debbie's dad had hold of her and they just went in and left me standing there as if I was invisible or summat, so I came home.'

'It's that nut-case again,' said Carole flatly. 'She'll be dead by now.'

'Carole!' Her mother glared at her. 'Don't talk like that. You don't know. She might have gone off with a friend. To a party or something. Why do some folk always have to look on the black side?'

Their dad stuck his head round the door. 'I've done some sausage and chips but I thought we'd wait till Mick and Dale get in. Black side of what, love?'

His wife told him.

'Ah,' he said. 'Our Carole's probably right, y'know. Still, let's hope not, eh?' He went back into the kitchen.

'Where is our Dale, anyway?' asked Brian.

Carole shrugged. 'Dunno. He went out for some fags, but that was hours ago. I'm not waiting supper for him. I'm starving.'

Five minutes later Mick came in and his mother told him the story while her husband went backwards and forwards putting the supper out. There was no sign of Dale. When it was ready they sat round the table: all except Mick, who wrinkled up his nose and said, 'Not for me, thanks. When you've been frying all night you don't fancy owt fried.'

'No-one's forcing you,' growled his father.

'I've only spent an hour and a half getting it ready for you, that's all.'

Mick shrugged. 'Sorry, Dad. I just don't fancy it, OK?'

'Aye. You said.'

'You don't have to cook the supper, love,' his wife told him. 'I can see to it when I get in.'

'Oh aye!' His lip curled. 'I'd look a right 'un, wouldn't I? Sitting about all day and then letting my wife start cooking when she gets in from work. Talk sense, Renee.'

'There's no need to talk to me like that,' she cried. 'It's not my fault you haven't got a job. You've been like a bear with a sore head ever since that rotten factory shut down.'

'Aye, and you'd be like a bear with a sore head if you'd to sit and watch your wife and kids bringing the money in while you did sod-all. You don't know what it's like, Renee. Nobody does.' He filled his mouth and chewed savagely, aware of his family's eyes on him. He swallowed and said, 'I went down the post office today to cash my Giro, and George Barraclough shoved the money at me as if he were keeping me out of his own pocket. He didn't even look at me, let alone say owt, and I've known him twenty years.'

They picked at their food, apprehensive, waiting for him to continue. But he ate in silence for several minutes and when he spoke again he said, 'Anyway, at least we've not got a lass missing; that's summat to be thankful for.'

118

*'Aye,' murmured his wife, and the others nodded. We've a lad missing, though, thought Brian, but he kept the thought to himself. Somewhere, an ambulance was out. Its siren reached them faintly, like a thin wire stretched across the night.

4

'What we come round this way for; you treating me to a seat in t'stand or summat?'

It was Saturday: a raw afternoon in late November. Town, low in the table following a string of defeats, were at home to Bristol City. Brian and Lee had bumped into each other by chance and were making their way to the ground. They always went on the Kop, and normally took a route which led directly to the turnstiles at that end. Today, Brian had insisted on taking a long way round and Lee, mystified, had tagged along. They were walking along a street of derelict houses: one of several such streets which lay to the south of Hillside, awaiting demolition.

'No, am I hummer treating you in t'stand. I want to show you summat, that's all.'

The other boy looked at his watch. 'It's seven minutes to three. We'll miss kick-off if we're not careful.'

'Will we heck. There'll be no queue at the turnstiles after six defeats in a row, and getting knocked out of the cup by a non-league side. They might even wait for us.'

'What we looking at, anyway?'

'That.' Brian nodded towards a dilapidated house that looked no different from the forty or so others in the terrace, except that a strand of dirty pink tape hung from one of its doorposts. 'That's where they found Leanne Stanton.'

Lee gazed at the house. 'How d'you know?' he asked. His voice sounded husky.

'Gary Sparks' sister works at the police station. She gets to know all sorts. She was strangled with a piece of wire from the lamp factory.'

'Gary Sparks' sister?'

'No, you div! Leanne Stanton. They're looking for someone who worked there.'

'Nearly everyone in Barfax worked there.'

'I know. That's why they haven't got him yet. He did that other lass the same way and all – that Janet Stobbs.'

'In t'same house?'

'No. I don't think so, but it was somewhere round here. If I were them I'd put about fifty coppers on guard here all the time. Hidden in the houses. He's bound to do another. These nuts always do, and if they waited long enough they'd get him.'

'Can we go now?'

'Why – you scared or summat?'

'Am I heck. I want to see t'game, that's all.'

Town's luck didn't seem to have changed, because they were a goal down at half-time. Lee booted a bit of loose concrete across the crumbling terrace and said, 'Got a tin on you, Col?'

Colin nodded. 'D'you think it's all right, with the cameras and that?'

"Course. It's not illegal. Get it out.'

Jonathan rolled his eyes. 'Hear that, Jeannette – Colin's getting it out.'

Lee, Jonathan, and Jeannette went into a huddle round Colin and he pulled a tin of glue from his pocket. Illegal or not, it was probably better to block out the cameras' view. He took the tin out of its bag, unscrewed the cap and used a key to prise off the inner, airtight lid. He scooped a dollop of glue with the plastic tag on his keyring and shook it into the bag. Then he resealed the tin, returned it to his pocket and squatted, scraping the tag clean on the concrete as the huddle broke up. He stood up and buried his nose and mouth in the bag, inhaling deeply before passing it to Lee. Lee had a good sniff and handed it back. Colin offered it to Brian.

'Here, Brian – have a go.'

'No thanks. I'm not getting into that.'

'Why not?' Colin looked hurt. 'It's just the job for a boring game like this.' He laughed.

121

'The second half'll be a nail-biter for me, even if they come out and play bleedin' chess.'

'No thanks.'

Colin shrugged and held out the bag towards Jonathan. 'Here, Johnnie.'

Jonathan pulled a face. 'I don't want to, and if you make me I'll tell Dad.'

Colin clucked. 'What the heck's up with everybody? How about you, Jeannette?'

'Yeah. Might as well take a chance. Leanne Stanton did.'

Brian gave her a scandalized look. 'That's sick, Jeannette.'

'Aw shove it, Brian, will you? I thought you were changing your image when you did that car, but you're still a flippin' wally underneath.'

Brian didn't reply. He turned away and stood gazing across the pitch as they passed the gluebag round. Play re-started but he couldn't concentrate on it. Jeannette's words had stung him, and he was uncomfortably aware that she and the others were getting high, and that they were probably being watched. He hoped it wouldn't reach the stage where they didn't know what they were doing.

The game dragged on with no change in the score. The thin Barfax crowd, out-shouted by the visitors, gave little encouragement to their team and there was less than a minute to go when Dickie Lester cut out a pass in midfield and broke down the right with the Bristol defence well forward. He swerved infield and sent in a cracking shot from twenty-five metres. The ball stayed low, curving in the air to ricochet off the near post into the back of the net.

It was all over. Five minutes later Brian and the others had pushed and shoved their way out of the ground and were on their way home.

'How about that then, Brian?' slurred Lee. His eyes had a glazed look and his grin was slack. Brian looked at him.

'It were only a draw, y'know. Them other ten goals you saw came out of the gluebag.' Colin shouted with laughter and Jeannette joined in.

'I didn't see no ten goals,' protested Lee, 'but we got a point, didn't we? That's better than nowt.'

'Only just. One point from six games and kicked out of t'cup by Spennymoor. They want flogging.'

'It's you that wants flogging, you miserable sod,' sneered Jeannette. 'If you'd had a sniff like the rest of us you wouldn't be flippin' moaning.'

'It makes no difference though, does it? You're high now, but they'll still be in t'bottom four when you come down, and you'll still have them spots round your gob and all.'

'Listen who's talking!' flared Jeannette.

123

'You've got spots all over your cretinous face, you leper.'

'Hey!' Jonathan, worried by the growing acrimony of the exchange, tried to change the subject. 'Are we all off to Gillingham next week?'

'I won't be,' growled Brian. 'My mum got the electric bill this morning. Over a hundred quid. My dad says I've to tip up my paper money, so I'll have nowt.'

'I can't go either,' said Jeannette. 'I'm having my hair done Friday night and my mum's making me pay for it myself. It's eleven pound fifty.'

'Great,' growled Colin.

'Well that's it, innit?' said Lee. 'No brass, no jobs, we might get blown up any minute, Town's in t'bottom four and someone's doing lasses in, and they wonder why we get high. It might not be all that great, but it beats reality, dunnit?'

5

Lee Harrison is the eldest of eight children. His mother had him when she was seventeen. She's only thirty-two now but when she looks in the mirror she sees a hag of fifty. She doesn't look in the mirror much, and she doesn't clean up either. Not now. She has four-year-old twins who are into everything and she can't cope any more so she swallows green and black capsules from the doctor and sits in the chair, crying.

Her husband's called Lee, too. When she met him he was king of the Barfax Bike Boys. The three Bs. Now there are two more: Booze and Bed. Lee senior has been unemployed so long he'd have to look for work in the dictionary, and he doesn't give a toss. In fact, that's what he's famous for now that his biking days are over. 'That Lee Harrison,' those who know him are apt to say, 'he doesn't give a toss.'

Once, in his heyday, he found a pretty girl taking a short-cut across what it pleased him to think of as his territory. He persuaded her to pay him for the privilege and as a result he has a daughter he's never met. He doesn't know this, and probably never will. And if you're thinking he wouldn't give a toss if he did know, you're right.

Lee junior gets most of his own meals and goes to bed when he likes and is often tired at school. Evenings and weekends, he helps out at the garage down the road. It gives him a bit of pocket-money and gets him out of the house. Lee is ashamed of the house. He never lets his friends in, because he knows that callers notice the smell. The insurance man hovers in the doorway, refusing invitations to sit down while Mrs Harrison rummages in the drawer. He stands there, ignoring the twins and trying not to stare at the sticky upholstery, and Lee can tell by his expression that he is thinking, 'How can people live like this?'

As soon as he is sixteen, Lee plans to find a place of his own. It will not be anything like this place. Never. But in the meantime he is stuck. For now, this is Lee's reality.

6

Early in December, Ramsden's crew lugged out all the stuff they'd made and the drama hall became King Lear's palace. For the first time, the cast was able to rehearse among the backdrops and flats which would be used on the night, while the crew practised lighting, changes, and sound-effects.

Even now, however, the play didn't produce much contact between Debbie and Brian. Following Leanne's murder, Mr Baxter tried to withdraw his daughter from the production on the grounds that he wanted her home in daylight. Debbie protested strenuously, the drama teacher wrote to him, and finally a compromise was arrived at. Debbie would attend evening rehearsals, but she would have to leave at nine o'clock sharp because her father would be there with the car to drive her home.

When she told Brian, he was furious. 'I only volunteered for this flippin' lark so I could see you more, and now I'm seeing you less. Couldn't you tell him I'd be walking you home?'

Debbie shook her head. 'You know how he is about you. He'd say it might be you doing the murders or something like that.' She smiled, squeezing his arm. 'Anyway, there's still after school and backstage and Saturdays. They can't watch us all the time.'

December blew in on bitter, easterly winds. *Lear* improved, Barfax Town did not, and the killer remained at liberty. One afternoon Leanne's parents called at the school, and the next morning in assembly Old Dodgson announced that *Lear* would run, not for one night, but three. Admission would be charged, and the proceeds used to buy a trophy to be known as the Leanne Stanton Cup.

This would be presented annually to the girl or boy who, in the judgement of staff and older pupils, had contributed most to the quality of life within the school community.

'I think it's a great idea,' said Debbie, as she and Brian dawdled home that afternoon. 'I nearly burst out crying.'

Brian nodded. 'Aye. It was a bit like that. Anyway, it makes it more worthwhile, doesn't it? The play I mean. There's some point to it now.' He grinned ruefully. 'P'raps Colin and them'll stop getting on at me about it now.'

She smiled. 'Have they been getting on at you?'

'Oh aye. Calling me Ken Branagh and stuff like that. Maybe they'll leave it out now that it's all for Leanne, like. It is a nice idea.'

'Yes.' Debbie was silent for a while, and there was a catch in her voice when she added, 'I'd rather have old Leanne, though.'

7

The play was a roaring success. Its cause ensured a good write-up in the local rag and packed houses on all three nights. On the second night, to Brian's amazement, his parents came. Debbie's folks were there every night. The final performance was attended by the Lord Mayor and Lady Mayoress. The acting was superb, the changes went like clockwork and the storm was a beauty. Mrs Stanton wept on her husband's shoulder as the civic dignitaries led a standing ovation which continued through three curtain-calls.

Backstage, Ramsden grinned at his tired crew. 'They get all the glory,' he hissed, 'but you did all the work. Greasepaint's all very well but it's no good without sweat. Well done.'

After, in the half-light, among props, painted canvas, and discarded costumes, Debbie and Brian snatched a moment together, high on the afterglow of triumph.

'Listen.' Debbie clasped her hands behind his neck and pulled him down till their foreheads touched. 'Have a good Christmas, right?' She was going away tomorrow with her parents. 'And give me a ring on the twenty-eighth. And cheer up and all, because you never know – next year could be a good 'un.'

'Aye. Well it couldn't be much worse than this one, could it? Not unless the Provos get us.'

'Knickers to the Provos. You might win the Lottery. Get discovered. Anything!'

'Sure.' He hugged her. 'You were magic tonight, Deb. I wish you weren't going away.'

'I didn't feel magic when I was lying there pretending to be dead, and Unsworth was saying all that about me being gone for ever and doing the feather bit. It was only then I remembered Leanne's mum and dad were there. It must have made them feel rotten.'

'Oh, I dunno. I expect they know the play anyway. Knew it was coming, I mean.'

'I hope so. Anyway look.' She broke his embrace and squinted at her watch in the gloom. 'Mum and Dad'll be waiting. I'd better go.'

He grinned. 'OK. See you, Cordelia.'

'Not if I see you first, scene-shifter.'

He hung about till everybody had gone, then set off home. He didn't want company. He wasn't depressed or anything. Quite the reverse in fact. For the first time in weeks he felt good. He just wanted to walk slowly and savour it. It had been terrific tonight, and maybe Debbie was right. Maybe the new year would be better. He smiled to himself. Maybe Rickstraw would score a goal. After all, accidents do happen.

The house was dark as he opened the gate, as if everyone was out or in bed. He looked at his watch. Ten past ten. He went up the path and tried the side door. It opened. Mick stood grinning with a lighted candle in his fist.

'They cut the electric off,' he said. 'Merry Christmas.'

8

It wasn't as bad as it might have been. By Christmas Eve the power had been off for two days and they'd got used to wearing outdoor clothing indoors, washing in cold water and moving about at night by the half-light of torches and candles. At six o'clock there was a knock on the door. It was Mrs Barker from next door. 'How are you managing for cooking?' she said, standing in the cold, dim kitchen with her cardigan round her shoulders.

'We're not,' Brian's mum told her. 'We're making do with cold stuff.'

'But what about the bairn?' she asked. 'And Christmas dinner; you're never going to give them a cold Christmas dinner?' Mrs Barker was from the north-east and spoke with a rising inflection which Brian found attractive

Mrs Gower laughed. 'We haven't much choice, love. You can't cook a turkey over a candle. Ken's got one of them tinned ones – they're ready cooked and there's no bones.'

'Eee!' The woman shook her head. 'It's wicked, that's what it is. Leaving folks without heat and light, and them with kids and all. Talk about Scrooge. I'd have ye all round my place but there's a houseful already.'

'Don't you worry, love,' said Ken. 'We're all right.' He grinned. 'There wasn't any electricity in that stable, y'know.'

'No,' Mrs Barker replied, 'but you haven't got a star, have you?'

'Nor three wise men neither,' said Carole, cuddling her son in her lap.

'One'd do,' put in Mick. He was on a day off, and for once was missing the greasy fug of the Chicken Shack. 'Him with the gold.' Everybody laughed.

'There's one thing I can do, mind,' said their neighbour. 'I can cook your meat and veg tomorrow, and make you a nice drop of gravy. And I think my man's got one of those gas things somewhere – those camping stoves. It'll only take a saucepan mind, but at least you'll be able to brew tea. I'll get him to look for it.'

The camping stove duly appeared, and the Gowers started Christmas Day with boiled eggs, tea, and carols on the radio. 'Don't chuck that water away,' growled Dad, as his wife scooped eggs from the pan. 'I'll have a shave with that.'

After breakfast they opened their presents and helped little Nicholas open his. Brian and Mike heated another pan of water and washed up, and then everybody sat with their coats on, talking and smoking and listening to the radio.

At nine o'clock Dale found two crumpled ten pound notes on the mat in the hall, and at half-past ten Mrs Barker came round for the turkey and vegetables. Mrs Gower thrust the notes under her nose. 'Did you push these through my letter-box?'

The woman shook her head. 'I didn't, pet. I've none to spare. Maybe it was Father Christmas.' She picked up the plastic carrier.

'I'll have these ready at twelve. Send one of the lads round.'

When Brian returned with the meal at five past twelve, they found that Mrs Barker had included some slices off her own bird, together with some sausages and a slab of sage and onion stuffing.

In the afternoon the Queen's message was on the radio. 'I wonder if their electric's on?' said Brian.

It turned a bit colder after tea and little Nick started wittering, so Carole put him to bed. Mr Gower would normally have gone off to his local on Christmas night, but he wouldn't go this time. 'Nay,' he said. 'I'd look well, wouldn't I – supping in a nice warm pub while my wife and kids sit at home shivering. It'd be like one of them songs the Band of Hope used to sing.'

It got colder as the evening wore on, and at ten o'clock Mick made them all some cocoa. 'I suppose,' he said, as they sat with their hands wrapped round the hot mugs, 'this has been what they call a good old-fashioned family Christmas.'

'Aye,' said Brian. 'And they can stuff it. Roll on tomorrow's game.'

9

It was a great occasion. The weather was bitter, but the traditional Boxing Day fixture had brought the crowd out. For the first time since Town met Liverpool at home in the cup four years ago, there were more than ten thousand at Hillside. They were wrapped in scarves, caps, and gloves they'd got as presents the day before, and a lot of them had flat bottles tucked in their inside pockets with a nip or two of Scotch or brandy against the cold. There was a great deal of what the commentators call atmosphere.

Even the Ointment were in good humour. Barry Weatherall had been arrested at the last home game and had appeared in court in the interim. He'd been fined a hundred pounds and the case had been reported in the *Telegraph*. One of his cronies had brought a clipping. As the crowd waited for the game to start, this lad produced his clipping and proceeded to read it out in a town-crier's voice for the entertainment of his companions. He read so loudly that he could be heard clearly in most parts of the ground, and people looked in his direction, enjoying the Ointment's largely feigned mirth.

'Nigel Robert Weatherall,' the reader cried. The Ointment roared, pointing at Barry and falling about. 'Shurrup!' growled Weatherall, prevented by the cameras and the warning he'd received in court from retaliating in the usual way. 'Just shurrup, will you?' But they repeated his forenames in raucous tones and his voice was drowned by theirs. 'Nigel Robert,' they spluttered, hanging onto one another for support. 'Nigel-pillocking-Robert-cowing-Weatherall!'

'Shurrup!' snarled Weatherall. 'You might be all right in here but there's no cameras outside. I'll have the lot of you after.'

'When cautioned,' continued the reader, straining to make himself heard, 'defendant told the arresting officer, "You want to get a grip of your knickers and catch the – dash – who's doing them lasses in." They've printed a dash there.'

'He must have said a naughty word,' said Aziz.

'Aye!' cried a curly-haired youth in denim. 'It'd be "bounder". I bet you said "catch the bounder" didn't you, Nigel? Didn't you, Nigel Robert Quentin St John Weatherall, eh? Admit it, you cad.'

Walsall ran on to the field, cutting short the merriment, and three minutes later the game began.

It was one of those days when it seems a team can do no wrong. Straight from kick-off, Cook went streaking down the left and lofted the ball to Harris who'd made a good run up the middle. Harris controlled it and tapped it on for Lester who ran it into the penalty area. He rounded one defender and was steadying himself to shoot when another charged in and, making no attempt to go for the ball, hacked his legs from under him. Lester rolled about in agony and the home crowd roared as the referee pointed to the spot.

Harris sent the goalie the wrong way, and it was one–nil. The game was forty-five seconds old. Within thirteen minutes Town were three up, delighted fans were asking one another why the team couldn't play like this all the time, and the Ointment were chanting, 'We want ten.'

It was four–nil at half-time. Brian and Jonathan bought hot Cornish pasties and stood, stamping their frozen feet and gasping, as the food burned their mouths.

'What we should do,' mumbled Jonathan through a mouthful of scalding mush, 'is send a bucket round. The Brian Gower Electricity Appeal. There's about ten thousand people here. If everybody put ten pee in, we'd have a thousand quid. You could pay the electric and I could have four weeks in the Bahamas.'

'If they play like this,' said Brian, 'I'm not bothered about the electric. They can leave it off for me.'

The second half was a jamboree. Relieved of all pressure, Barfax turned on an exhibition, and with five minutes to play and the score at six–nil, the exhibition culminated in a miracle. Lyle floated a ball across from the right and the hapless Walsall keeper, under severe pressure, attempted to punch it clear. His fist clipped the ball, deflecting it sharply downwards. It fell at the feet of Rickstraw, who was standing just outside the six yard box thinking about his girlfriend. Seeing the thing inches from his toes, and worried lest its proximity cause someone to tackle him, he lashed out and sent it skittering into the right-hand corner of the net.

So unexpected was this occurrence that there was a moment of stunned silence before the roar. 'Blimey!' whispered Colin. 'It must've gone in off God.'

'*Sev'n nil, se-heven nil, sev'n nil, sev'n nil . . .*' sang the Ointment, to the appropriate tune of 'Amazing Grace'.

The final whistle blew, and with a fat roar of festive satisfaction the crowd turned and surged towards the exits. Brian draped one arm round Colin's neck and the other round Lee's and allowed them to half carry him, laughing and singing, across the Kop.

10

January was one of the coldest on record. It snowed on the night of the second, and frost every night thereafter kept the stuff deep and crisp and even, except in the streets of the town where it became a semi-frozen mush which looked like brown sugar and had a way of seeping through the welts of all but the most expensive footwear.

The icy wind which keened night after night about the Gower house seemed to suck out the last vestiges of comfort until it became impossible to keep warm except in bed. Ken Gower wrote to the Electricity Board, explaining that the family was saving as best it could to pay off the arrears and meet the re-connection charge, but that in the meantime they were having a hard struggle to keep Carole's baby warm.

He might as well not have bothered. Eight days later he received a single, brief para-graph of gobbledegook, the gist of which was that the Board was unwilling to make an exception in their case. Ken pictured some smug official in an overheated office, dictating the thing in a bored voice before passing on to something more important.

Halfway through the month, Nick devel-oped a chesty cough. In desperation, Renee

Gower went to see her mother and persuaded the old lady to take Carole and the child till the cold spell broke. They left on the sixteenth, but this time nobody moved into the empty bedroom. It was warmer in a huddle.

With the holidays over, Brian and Debbie continued to walk home from school together but it had become impossible for Debbie to slip out in the evenings. The police seemed to be getting nowhere in their hunt for the murderer, and if she had to go anywhere after six her father took her by car.

The freeze was virtually countrywide and the League programme was badly hit. Brian didn't mind. The cash from his paper round was going into the kitty anyway, and postponed games would be played later when he might have the cash to attend. In the one game they did manage to play, away to Plymouth Argyle, Town were thrashed six–nil and so Brian wished it had not taken place.

'I reckon the only chance we've got of staying in t'Second division is if this turns out to be the start of another ice-age,' he said.

11

'Deb!' Mr Baxter covered the mouthpiece with his hand and called up the stairs. 'Telephone.'

The dulcet tones of Madonna faded as his daughter operated the volume control. She looked over the bannister.

'Who is it?'

'I don't know, love. Some fella. Come on.'

Debbie ran down the stairs and took the receiver. 'Hello?' Her father seemed inclined to linger. She made a go-away motion with her head and he moved off, looking unhappy.

'Debbie Baxter?' She didn't recognize the voice. There was something odd about it.

'Yes. Who's that?'

'Never mind. Listen. Stay away from Royston Ambler.'

'I haven't been anywhere near Royston Ambler. Is that you, Brian?' Brian had never mentioned his abortive clash with Ambler, but she'd heard about it from somebody else.

'I told you – it doesn't matter who I am. Just stay away from him. It's for your own good.'

'It is Brian, isn't it?' She was becoming angry. 'If you've got something to say to me, why don't you say it face to face instead of making stupid phone-calls through your hanky or whatever it is? I don't think it's funny, Brian, and I don't like being told what to do.'

The caller laughed briefly: more like a yap

than a laugh. 'You're right about one thing, young woman. It's not funny. Not in the least. And there are worse things than being told what to do, as you may learn to your cost if you choose not to heed this warning. Goodbye.'

There was a clatter and then the dialling tone. Debbie stood staring at the receiver in her hand. Her raised voice had brought her father out again. He nodded towards the phone. 'Who was it – what's the matter, love?'

'I – dunno. A funny voice, telling me to stay away from Royston Ambler.' She replaced the receiver, clumsily because she was trembling. 'It might have been Brian but I'm not sure.'

'Well whoever it was it's a damned silly trick, frightening people like that. Go in and sit down and I'll make you some coffee. Have you been seeing the Ambler boy, Deb?'

'No. I told you. He's too old. Why would anybody want to . . .'

'Forget it, love, eh?' He put an arm round her and steered her towards the sitting-room. 'It was probably one of those idiots who get their kicks by making sick calls. Did he say anything else – anything dirty?' Debbie shook her head.

'Well look – I'll get you that coffee, and then I've got to go and pick your mother up. Will you be all right, or do you want to come with me?'

She sat down, shivering, holding out her

hands to the gas fire. 'I'm all right, Dad, thanks. But if it turns out it was that Brian Gower, I'll kill him.'

12

'It wasn't me, Deb – honest. I wouldn't do owt like that. D'you believe me?'

It was twenty to nine. They huddled under the bike-shed with scarves round their ears while the wind blew sleet across the yard.

'I don't know whether I believe you or not. You never told me about that fight you had down Giggles.'

Brian looked at her sharply. 'How'd you know about that?'

She shrugged. 'It doesn't matter. But if it wasn't you, who could it have been – who else gives a damn if I go out with Royston or not?'

'Like your dad said. Probably just some nut. But it wasn't me, Deb. I wish I could prove it to you.'

'Well you can't.' She smiled. 'I think I believe you though. I just hope whoever it was doesn't ring again, that's all.'

'Well – that's up to you really, isn't it?'

'How d'you mean?'

He grinned. 'If you stay away from Royston Ambler he won't need to ring again, will he?'

Brian was fast, but Debbie was faster. She caught him by the staff car park and shoved an icy slushball down his neck.

13

The cold spell dragged on into February, making life uncomfortable for the Gowers. With the baby safe and warm elsewhere, they learned to use what little they had to the best advantage and make do. Neighbours chipped in with the odd pot of tea or flask of soup but there were no more ten pound notes. The closure of the lamp factory had hit the town hard and everybody was in the same boat.

In spite of everything the kitty grew. On the seventeenth Sharon, Brian's married sister, drove over and passed a hundred pounds into her mother's hand. 'Call it a loan if you like,' she said, 'but there's no rush about paying it back.'

Added to what they'd scraped together, this made two hundred and eighty pounds. As soon as Sharon had gone, her parents piled into the old banger and drove through the snow and slush to the Electricity showrooms.

'I expect it'll take five weeks and forms in triplicate before you can get it back on again,' said Ken to the clerk, but he was wrong. An engineer arrived at half-past eight the following morning.

'Ta,' said Ken, when the man had reconnected the supply. 'If I'd known it was as easy as that I'd have done it myself weeks ago.'

The engineer shook his head. 'It wouldn't have been advisable,' he said. 'It's dangerous if you don't know what you're doing and of course it's against the law.'

'It isn't against the law to let little kids and pensioners die of hypothermia because they've no brass though, is it?' said Ken.

The engineer grew defensive. 'I wouldn't know about that. I'm only an employee, same as you.'

'I'm not an employee,' Ken told him. 'I'm an unemployee. That's why I couldn't pay. Have you any idea what it's been like in this house all through January?'

'I can imagine.'

'No you can't. Nobody can, unless they've been through it. I know it's not your fault, mate, but that's the trouble – you can never get to them that make the rules. They should live like we've lived for a bit. They'd soon change the rules then, I can tell you.'

'I'm sure you're right. Anyway, I'd better be off – I've nine more to do before twelve. Good morning.'

It was a good morning. They had the heat on before the man was back in his van. They capered about, whooping and laughing, touching the radiators till they felt it gurgling through. Mrs Gower ran upstairs to feel the cylinder while Brian and Mick switched on the TV and sat, feasting their eyes on the movement and the colour.

When everybody had calmed down a bit Mick said, 'I know. Let's have a party!'

'Aye,' said his father, 'a house-warming party. It's Giro day and all. Dale and me'll call in at Morrison's and the take-away on the way back so nobody has to start cooking. Come on, Dale.'

It was a fine party. The only guests were the television set, the washing machine and the radiators. The Gowers ate, drank and were merry. The TV flashed and blared. The washing machine hummed and the radiators glowed. A fine party.

Oh – there was one other guest. It was a forgotten guest and so it had to amuse itself, clicking and whirring in the cubby-hole under the stairs. Its name was meter. Peter the meter if you like, and it had a friend called Bill who always showed up when the party was over.

14

*'Happy Birthday, dear Brian;
Happy Birthday to you!'*

Everybody clapped. Brian smiled and nodded and got to work on the little pile of packages and envelopes beside his plate.

It was breakfast time on the sixteenth of March and Brian was sixteen. The big freeze had given way to wet, windy weather and his life lately had consisted of swotting for exams and grieving for his team, now languishing second from the bottom in Division Two. There was Debbie of course, but it was becoming harder for them to meet and his birthday came as a splash of colour on a field that was mostly grey.

There were the usual cards from grandparents, aunts and uncles, as well as the immediate family. There was one from Debbie too. Feeling a bit daft, he read out the soppy verses and stood them up in a semicircle. 'Eleven!' his mother exclaimed. 'You've done well, our Brian.'

'Aye, I know.' She said the same thing every birthday.

'Open your pressies, then.'

He opened his presents. There was a sweatshirt and trainers from Mum and Dad and the new Blur album from Mick. Carole, staying on with Grandma Phillips, had sent a book which had a lurid cover and looked like a murder mystery. His married sister had pinned a Marks and Sparks voucher to her card. It had fallen to Dale – poor old Dale, thought Brian in spite of what he'd done to that harmless shopkeeper – to provide this year's sad present. Why does there always have to be one sad present? he wondered. Kindly meant but mistakenly chosen: the sort of present that makes you feel like crying, not for yourself but for the giver? Dale had bought him an enormous, glossy poster of a band he'd been keen on about two years ago, but which now he didn't give a damn about: a band whose CDs he'd recently given away, in fact. The big daft lump had probably blown all his fag money on it, and he'd sat there grinning as Brian pulled it out of the tube and unrolled it.

He held the thing open, looked at it with what he hoped would pass for admiration and grinned across the table at his brother. 'Thanks, our Dale,' he said. 'It's an ace picture.' There was a familiar lump in his throat.

He was halfway through his cornflakes when the newsreader on the breakfast TV show said something about Barfax Town.

'Sssh!' He put his spoon down. Everybody stopped talking and looked at the screen. It was a still shot of Hillside, with Seth Ambler's face in a box. '– already deep in trouble as the season draws to a close, is to lose its

Chairman. Mr Seth Ambler, a prominent local businessman, announced his resignation last night during a crisis meeting at the Hillside ground. Afterwards, he spoke to our reporter, Martin Carthy.'

The scene shifted to an office. Ambler was sitting behind a desk with a mike clipped to his tie. 'Mr Ambler,' said the reporter. 'A lot of Town supporters will be watching this programme. Can you tell them what led to this decision?'

'Well,' Ambler's eyes kept swivelling to the monitor. He looked rough. 'There are a number of factors, but my health's the main one. As you know I lost my wife three years ago, and I haven't been completely well since. I sold my business on the advice of my doctor but the winter has further undermined my constitution and now I feel it's time to make way for a younger man. Time to move on – hopefully to somewhere a bit warmer.' He smiled, wanly.

'I know somewhere a bit warmer you could go,' growled Brian. His mother frowned at him.

The reporter spoke again. 'Town are deep in trouble, Mr Ambler. It seems they're bound for the Third Division, and there are sure to be those who will interpret your action as deserting the sinking ship. What would you say to those people?'

The interview continued, but Brian wasn't interested. 'The rat!' he muttered, screwing a piece of wrapping-paper into a tight ball. 'The fat, stinking rat. Just when we're struggling. Just when we need everybody pulling together. You'd think he'd done enough damage wouldn't you, putting everybody out of work, without taking our soccer away and all?'

'He's not taking it away,' said his mother quietly. 'It'll go on, even if it is in the Third Division. And you've got to admit he looks poorly.'

'Poorly?' Brian hurled the ball of paper at the waste-paper basket. It missed and rolled under the sideboard. 'He'll look poorly if the Ointment get hold of him.' He looked around the table. Everybody was watching him and he felt a pang. They'd done their best to give him a good birthday and here he was moaning and groaning. It wasn't their fault that Town were in the bottom four, or that Ambler was a wally. He got his presents together and stood up. 'Thanks, everybody,' he smiled. 'I mean it.'

'Happy birthday, love,' said his mother. 'And many of 'em.'

15

As soon as Brian walked into the arcade, Debbie ran to him and threw her arms round his neck.

'Vulcan Pan's opening this new supermarket at Marley,' she said. 'It's at three o'clock. You'll come with me, won't you?' Her eyes shone. He sensed her excitement. His heart quailed at the prospect of disappointing her, but he was going to have to. Town were at home to Bury in the last match of the season.

Bury were lying fifth from the foot of the table with thirty-two points, and Town were one place below on thirty-one. Town had to win today to stay in Division Two. To lose would send them down. So would a draw. It was the most vital game in the club's history. He took hold of Debbie's wrist, broke her grip gently and, without letting go, shook his head.

'I can't, Deb. I'm sorry.'

'Why? Why can't you?' She twisted her hands about, trying to get free of him. 'It's that stupid football again, isn't it? You can go to football any Saturday but Vulcan Pan's only here once. You know I'm mad on him. Can't you forget football just this once, Brian – for me?'

He let go her wrists. 'No, Deb, I can't. It's the last game, and if Town don't win they're down. They've been playing so lousy I don't think they're going to do it. Anyway they'll need all the support they can get, and I've got to be there.'

'Go then!' she flared. 'And you can find someone else to go out with and all, 'cause that's it as far as I'm concerned. All this time I've lied and twisted and got myself in trouble to get out and see you, and the first time I ask you to do summat for me you chuck it back in my face. Get that Jeannette to go out with you, or any other slag for all I care, and I'll find someone to take me to Marley. Ta-ta, Brian. I hope they lose ten–nil.'

'Hey – hang on a minute, Deb. Don't . . .'

'Huh!' She turned with a toss of the head and walked rapidly away. He gazed after her and his eyes filled with tears as he felt himself torn between his loyalty to Barfax Town and an almost irresistible urge to run after her. He remembered a similar situation at Giggles. He'd made the wrong decision that time, and it had led to pain and humiliation. Was he making the same mistake again? Ought he to catch her, now, before it was too late? Take her to see Vulcan Pan if that was what she wanted. He could take his tranny – listen to the game on The Pulse. It was the same, wasn't it?

No, it wasn't. He bit his lip and wiped his eyes with the back of his hand. When he could see again, she'd gone.

Well, let her go then. Let her find someone

else. A lass who doesn't understand why he has to be at Hillside today of all days isn't worth bothering about. What was that Barry said? Rule your floggin' life if you give 'em half a chance. He was right, and all. Vulcan puff-puff Pan! That'll be the day. He left the arcade and walked round town in the pale April sunshine.

He felt vaguely uneasy. There was a sense of foreboding, and he kept fancying he'd either lost something or forgotten to do something. I've got the jitters, he told himself.

He popped into a newsagents and bought twenty Benson and Hedges and a box of matches. He didn't usually smoke, but cigarettes were supposed to calm your nerves and that was all that was wrong with him: nerves. He was getting himself into a state, thinking about the game. After the run they'd been having lately he couldn't see Town winning, but he couldn't imagine them not winning either. Surely, when it comes to the crunch and you need a win to stay up, you get it. You make sure you do. Especially when you're at home, and the side you're playing is only one point in front.

He sat on a bench in the market square, smoking and watching the shoppers. He could tell by looking at them that most of them didn't even know it was crunch day for Town, and that most of them wouldn't give a damn if they did. He couldn't imagine that.

When he was on his fourth fag, a bunch of Bury supporters went by in scarves and caps. They were laughing and horsing around, and when they'd gone Brian felt worse than before. They'd seemed too carefree; too confident. As if the game were a formality; its outcome a foregone conclusion. A feeling of doom washed over him and he shivered. 'We're going to lose,' he murmured. 'I can feel it.'

After a while he got cold just sitting. He looked across the square. The Shoulder of Mutton was open, so it must be half-past eleven. He glanced at his watch to confirm it, stubbed out his cigarette on the back of the seat and stood up. People were going into the pub. Some had Town scarves on, and some didn't look any older than him. He glanced around to check there was nobody who knew his parents, and slipped inside.

16

It seemed to Debbie that everybody in Barfax had decided to go to Marley. The queue stretched halfway across the bus station and it was only one o'clock. Most were young people, but there was a middle-aged couple in front of Debbie. The man was grumbling about the queue. After a while his wife turned to Debbie and said, 'Is there summat going on at Marley, love?'

Debbie nodded. 'Vulcan Pan's opening a new supermarket.'

'Ah.'

The man stared at her crossly. 'Duncan who?'

'Not Duncan,' said Debbie, 'Vulcan Pan. He's a pop star.'

'Aye, I dare say with a name like that. It's ridiculous. They should've put a special on for you lot.'

The woman smiled to make up for her husband's rudeness. 'You see, we go over every Saturday, love. For the market. And there's never any queue for the bus. Willie were a bit capped when he saw all these. He du'n't like queuing.'

'I don't either,' Debbie told her. 'A special would've been a good idea.'

'They haven't imagination for that,' grumbled Willie. He reminded Debbie of Norah Batty's husband.

The buses were every half-hour. One came in, filled up and went. Everybody shuffled forward. 'I bet we don't get on t'next 'un either,' said Willie. His wife gave him a baleful stare. 'Shut your gob, you miserable old gimmer.'

Willie and his wife got on the next one but Debbie didn't. She was on the step when the driver craned over Willie's head and said,

'That's all, love. There's another one coming.'

'Aye,' growled a voice in the queue. 'In half an hour.'

It wasn't half an hour. The bus company had noticed that something unusual was going on, and squeezed in a special. Debbie was first on. She sat looking out of the window, thinking about Brian. She hadn't found anyone to go with her. She'd never intended to, really. Brian would have made it fun, even in the queue. She wasn't going to change her mind though. Not this time. Brian was OK but he was too selfish. They always had to do what he wanted to do. He never considered her. And when it came to rotten football he was fanatical, like it was his religion or something. Anyway, she told herself, that's all in the past now.

It was two o'clock when the bus got to Marley. Debbie didn't know where the new supermarket was, but a stream of youngsters was moving along the main street and she tagged along. She hadn't walked far when the procession merged into a noisy throng and, by standing on tiptoe, she was able to see a large, empty car park and a long, low structure of dark-red brick with tinted windows and a blue ribbon stretched across its entrance. It was eleven minutes past two.

It was dinner time, but Brian decided not to go home. He'd had a pint of bitter and was starting on his second. There'd been no problem. Not like Giggles. The Shoulder of Mutton was packed and smoky and the two women behind the bar were either too busy to notice how young he was, or else they didn't care. He found a space on a ledge to put his glass on, and lit a cigarette.

He was feeling better. There were a lot of Town fans in, and they seemed every bit as cheerful as the Bury supporters he'd seen, so maybe he'd been wrong. Maybe there was nothing to worry about.

Except Debbie. He was worried about her all right. He'd never seen her so mad. Barry Weatherall wouldn't have worried. He'd have forgotten her by now, but Brian couldn't. Not yet, anyway. He took a pull of his beer and held the glass up, looking through it. Maybe after a couple more of these . . .

Vulcan Pan was five minutes late but nobody cared. As he emerged, grinning and waving, from his white Rolls-Royce, the crowd pressed forward against the low metal barriers, squealing and waving back. A girl with a Vulcan Pan T-shirt and an autograph book tried to climb over the barrier and had to be restrained by a policewoman. Debbie, five layers back, stood on tiptoe and craned her neck, steadying herself by resting her hands on the shoulders of the girl in front, who didn't seem to notice.

The pop star took it all in his stride. He was tall and thin, with a mane of pale hair and tight leather jeans. Flanked by a pair of burly minders, he spoke briefly into a PA system, thanking the supermarket company for having invited him and the crowd for having turned out to watch. Then he moved over to the doorway, somebody handed him a pair of scissors and, with a grin and some words which few of the spectators heard, cut the tape.

Everybody cheered. Vulcan Pan smiled and waved, then went over and leaned on the bonnet of the Rolls and signed photos of himself for his ecstatic admirers.

Debbie wasn't an autograph hunter, so she didn't join the long queue shuffling through the gap the police had made in the barrier. She stood for a while, gazing wistfully at her idol as he smiled and nodded and scribbled, then she sighed and turned away, joining the stream of people heading for the bus station. It had been terrific, seeing Vulcan in the flesh, and she was glad she'd come, but she didn't fancy the journey back. There'd be a massive queue for the bus again, and there was no guarantee that the company would lay on any more specials.

She was trailing along, wondering how long she'd have to wait, when she noticed that a green mini, which was being driven very close to the kerb, seemed to be keeping pace with her. As she noticed it, the driver leaned across, wound down the window and smiled at her.

'Heading for Barfax, love?' he asked. It was Royston Ambler.

19

'Hey up – here he comes.' Brian's friends watched as he made his way towards them. He didn't call out, and seemed unsteady on his feet. As he joined them, Lee said, 'Where the heck you been – you look like a treeful of owls.'

Brian shook his head. 'Nowhere,' he slurred. 'I've been nowhere.'

'He's drunk!' cried Colin. 'Pissed as a parrot, aren't you, mate?' He ruffled Brian's hair.

'Gerroff!' Brian swiped at his friend's hand and nearly fell over. 'I'm not, no. I've had a couple of pints, that's all.' He steadied himself and looked round. 'Good crowd.'

Jeannette laughed. 'That's 'cause you're seeing double, you div.'

'No I'm not. We're gonna thrash 'em today, aren't we, Lee? Staying up, aren't we?'

''Course!' said Lee.

It was seven minutes to three. The Ointment was belting out its version of 'Lord of the Dance'.

'Dance, dance, whoever you may be,
We're not bound for Division Three.
And we'll lead you all, whoever you may be,
And we'll never play in Division Three.'

Brian was starting to feel ill. He'd had breakfast before his paper-round and had eaten nothing since, and the combined effect of alcohol and nicotine on his empty stomach was too much.

He'd read somewhere that people drink to forget, but it hadn't worked for him. He'd thought about Debbie nearly all the time in the pub, and he was thinking about her now. Her, and the cruel game to come. And that was another thing. Fags are supposed to relax you, but Brian had smoked about ten and he still felt like a cat on hot bricks.

The teams took the field. The singing stopped. Everybody waited for the officials. There was atmosphere but it wasn't good. It was strained. Brittle. Everybody was thinking, this is it. Now. In an hour and a half, we'll know. You could feel it.

The game began. At first it was anti-climactic, as crunch games often are. The sides were cautious. Bury, needing only a draw, defended as though their manager had said, 'Nil–nil will do, lads.' Perhaps he had. Town could probably have pressured them in those early minutes but they didn't. For ten minutes they sparred. For fifteen. For twenty. The Barfax fans grew restive. They shuffled about, and there were shouts of 'Get on with it!'

'They're doing all right,' breathed Lee, but Brian shook his head and drew on his cigarette.

It was twenty-three minutes before Town mounted a real attack. They built it slowly, patiently: stringing together a series of shrewd, accurate passes which rang alarm bells in the minds of the Bury defenders and drew them out to challenge. Dickie Lester had the ball. He beat a defender and ran with the roar of the crowd in his ears, straight up the middle. The team came up in support. Lyle ran into space just outside the penalty area and called for the ball. Harris was there too, unmarked on the left. Lester dodged a tackle and passed to Lyle, and then it all went wrong. Instead of having a go, Lyle turned and punted the ball across the area. It was meant for Harris, but the move was obvious and a defender was on it like a flash, intercepting and passing to his winger with practically the whole Barfax side floundering. The crowd's excitement turned to dismay as the Bury winger streaked along the line and curved infield with only the goalie to beat.

MacNee came out to narrow the angle but it was too late. His opponent jinked and side-footed the ball past him into the net.

The home fans ground their teeth as the wild cheering of the Bury supporters gave way to a cruel chant.

'Going down, going down, going down . . .'

'Shurrup!' snarled Lee, digging his nails into his palms. 'Shurrup, you thick, stupid bastards.'

'We'll pull one back,' murmured Jeannette, without conviction.

'Two,' moaned Colin. 'We need two.'

'Two's nowt,' said Jonathan defiantly. 'We'll end up getting five, won't we, Brian?'

Brian sucked the last of the smoke from his tab-end, threw it on the ground and shook his head, exhaling. 'Will we heck.' His voice was hoarse. 'We've thrown it away. Thrown it away.'

The goal seemed to inject new life into Bury.

Their play became fluid, their footwork magic as they pressed home attack after attack. Only the skill of MacNee kept them out, and the dejected Barfax fans knew they were lucky not to be three or four down when the whistle blew for half-time.

The teams trailed off the field. The Bury supporters clapped and cheered while the home fans stood silent.

'Jesus,' breathed Brian. 'Listen to them bastards. Where's the Ointment? Why don't they go shut 'em up?'

Colin shrugged. 'It's the cameras. No-one fancies getting barred for next season.'

'Why not?' spat Brian. 'Who wants to watch Third Division crap anyway?'

'We're not down yet,' said Lee. 'It's only one–nil. If everybody shouts like hell for 'em in the second half, they'll do it. No-one's been shouting.'

'What we need,' said Colin, 'is a snifter of the old happiness. Hang on.' He produced a tin of glue. 'Gather round.'

When he'd got a dollop in the bag and put the tin out of sight, he looked at Brian. 'How about it, man? You were doing your puritan bit last time, but you've got a skinful of ale and cancer in both lungs so you might as well feel good for once. Here.'

Brian shook his head. 'Beer and fags might get you in the end, but that stuff can kill first time.' He grinned, ruefully. 'And I don't want to die just yet, even if we do go down.'

20

Debbie smiled uncertainly and nodded. 'Yes. I'm off home. Why?' She knew why. Royston would offer to drive her, and why not? She was through with Brian, so she wasn't being disloyal. She was free: her own woman.

'I'll run you. I'm going anyway.'

'OK.' It would make up for last time, when he'd been concerned for her safety and she'd rebuffed him. 'Thanks.'

He stopped the car and pushed the door open for her. She climbed in and pulled it shut. She expected him to drive on at once, but he didn't. She looked at him. He smiled. 'Seatbelt. You should fasten it.'

'Oh, yes. Sorry.' She felt herself blush, fumbling with the catch. Gently, he took it out of her hand and snapped it home.

'There.'

'Thanks.'

He waited, watching in the mirror, then pulled out into the traffic. 'Been to see Vulcan Pan, have you?'

'Yes. You?'

He chuckled. 'No. Fancy him, do you?'

'I like him, yes.'

'Yes, but do you fancy him?'

'How d'you mean?'

'You know. Would you like to go out with him? On a date?'

She looked at him. He seemed amused. 'I – don't know. I suppose so, but it's never going to happen so I haven't really thought about it.'

'He's probably a poof anyway.'

She flushed. 'Why should he be?'

They stopped at lights. Royston shrugged. 'Most of them are. Especially the ones that look really macho. Funny, isn't it?'

'Dunno.' She wished they could talk about something else. 'You're going away, aren't you?'

He nodded, accelerating away from the lights. 'Yes, worse luck. The old man's idea. Getting a bit warm for him in these parts.'

'Warm? He said on telly he wanted somewhere warmer.'

Royston laughed. 'I didn't mean that. I meant things are getting difficult. He thinks we should get away – start again where nobody knows us.'

'Why? Is it because of the factory?'

'Partly. And then there's the football club. But mostly, it's me.'

She glanced at him. 'You?'

He nodded. 'I'm an embarrassment to him, I suppose you could say.'

'Oh.' She didn't care for the way this conversation was going either. She changed tack. 'Where are you moving to – somewhere nice?'

He shrugged. 'It'll be all right. One place is much the same as another to me.' He chuckled again. 'As long as there are girls, that is.'

'Girls?'

'Oh yes. Must have his girls y'know, old Royston.'

'Oh.' She didn't know what to say to this. It seemed that every topic of conversation led somewhere she didn't want to go. Maybe it was because he was older. 'Have you any brothers or sisters?' she asked, though she was pretty sure he hadn't. He shook his head.

'No. Who needs them? Give me girls anytime.'

She gave him another sidelong glance. He wasn't smiling now. Unease stirred in her and she moistened her lips with her tongue. 'All boys like girls, I suppose. Most boys anyway.'

'Not like me. Not the way I mean.' His voice sounded odd. They were at lights again, waiting to make a right turn. A red Suzuki jeep pulled up on their left with a middle-aged woman at the wheel. Debbie looked across. The woman turned her head and their eyes met. Debbie nearly rapped on the window – nearly called out, seeking the woman's help, but then the moment passed and she looked away. Stupid, she told herself. She was falling apart, just because she was in a car with an older boy who said he liked girls. So he liked girls. So what?

The lights changed. The Suzuki slid away. Royston waited until two cars went by, then swept right and changed up, accelerating. Debbie looked out. This wasn't the way. This wasn't where the buses came from Marley to Barfax. She looked at him.

'This isn't the way.' She tried to sound casual but she sounded nervous, even to herself. He smiled.

'It's my way,' he murmured.

21

The prannocks. The lousy, rotten pigs.

Brian blinked tears of frustration from his eyes and stared through the double barrier. Beyond it the Bury fans were capering on the terrace, pointing and chanting.

'Going down, going down, going down . . .'

'They want smashing,' he choked. 'Smashing. Why doesn't someone shut 'em up, eh?'

'Shurrup moaning, Brian,' slurred Colin. 'I've told you before – if you got a sniff or two of this inside you, you'd be less uptight.' He giggled. 'It's like anaesthetic. You fall asleep in the Second Division and when you wake up you've been transplanted into the Third. Try it.'

'No thanks, mate. With my luck, I'd be one of them that dies on the operating table.'

22

'Where are we going?' Debbie was frightened. She took no trouble to hide the fact because he knew. She knew he knew.

'Scenic route.'

'I don't want to. Let me out here, please.'

'Cool it. We're having a little ride, that's all.'

'Where to?'

They were driving along a wide road between new-looking factories and ware-houses. Debbie thought it might be Holmfield Industrial Estate but she wasn't sure. The premises were all closed and there was very little traffic.

'A place I know.'

'No.' She shook her head. 'I don't want to. I want to go home.' She wished she could see a police car.

'We're going to a place I know. After, if you behave yourself, I'll take you home.'

'Behave yourself? What does that mean?'

He laughed. 'What does it mean? It means doing what I tell you to do.'

'Like what?'

He shrugged again. 'Nothing much. Nothing you'd need a university education to do. You'll see. Oh – and you can forget that!' He noticed her hand on the door handle and leaned across, locking it. 'You'd be smashed to a pulp anyway. We're doing fifty.'

'I don't want to go with you. I want to go home.' She began to cry.

'Don't give me the waterworks,' he snarled. 'Crying just gets me mad. We're nearly there.'

Debbie looked out. They had left the industrial estate behind. The car was turning into a street of empty houses. There was a sign on the first house. Hillside Road. Hillside. They must have travelled in a big curve, ending up somewhere near the football ground. She glanced around. Away to the right she saw the floodlight pylons sprouting out of broken roofs. The car was lurching and bumping over uneven setts and pieces of debris. Hillside Road. This was where—

Sobbing, she fumbled for the seatbelt release. This was where they found Leanne. Near here. Hillside Terrace. She'd been seen getting into a car, and now Debbie knew beyond all doubt that it had been this car. This driver. With a cry of horror she flung herself from him, twisting at the waist, slamming her back against the door. She hadn't managed to release the belt and it held her, cutting into her left shoulder. There was a sensation of warmth in her upper thighs and she knew she was wetting herself.

The car stopped. Ambler twisted the key and pulled it out of the ignition. The engine died with a shudder. He looked at her.

'In a minute,' he said softly, 'we're going to get out of the car and go into that house there.' He nodded towards a house she couldn't see because it was behind her. She shook her head.

'No. I'm not going, I want to go home.'

'I told you. You can go home when you've done as I say. We're going to get out of the car, but first—' He groped in a door-pocket and pulled out a length of wire. Debbie's eyes widened. She screamed. He laughed. 'You're all right. I'm not going to strangle you. I'm going to tie your ankles a bit so you don't run. Here.'

He made a grab at her right leg. Debbie lifted both feet and lashed out, kicking his hand. He snatched it away, made a fist and drove it into her stomach. With a gasp of agony she jack-knifed, oblivious of everything except the fight to breathe. Ambler slid forward and crammed himself into the cramped space below the dash. Working rapidly, he wound the thin wire first round one ankle, then the other. By the time the pain had subsided enough for Debbie to breathe, he was back in his seat and she was hobbled. He leaned across her and unlocked the door.

169

Then he operated the release on the seatbelt.

'Right,' he said, breathing hard. 'Get out. And don't start yelling and screeching or I'll smash your skull with this.' He brandished a jack-handle under her nose. 'Go on.'

Debbie sat with her arms wrapped round her stomach and shook her head. The wire cut into her ankles and she was half-mad with fear, yet something told her she was safer in the car than in the house.

'No!' she gasped. 'I won't. I'll do what you want here but I'm not getting out.' Crazily, she remembered her mother's phrase for Ambler and his kind. Funny men. There are funny men about, she used to say. Don't take sweets. Don't get in cars. There are funny men about. Why didn't she say there are men who'll terrify you and tie you up and hit you in the stomach and then, when they've finished with you, strangle you with wire or bash your head in with jack-handles? If she had, I wouldn't be here now. Wouldn't be here now—

There was a sudden noise. A roar. She lifted her tear-stained face. Ambler laughed at the hope in her eyes. 'Football,' he said. 'It's the crowd. They'll not help you. Get out.'

She shook her head. In spite of her terror, her mind was working rationally. He can't get me out if I won't go. He can't push me out. There isn't room. And he daren't smash me with the jack-handle. Not inside his own car.

'Get out, you dirty little bitch!' He started hitting her: pumping his fists repeatedly into her head and chest, calling her filthy names. She doubled up, shielding herself as best she could with hands and elbows. It hurt. It hurt like hell, but it wasn't killing her.

Abruptly, the blows ceased. She peered at him through her fingers. He looked at his watch, then started making noises in his throat, almost like crying. He opened the door on his own side and swung his legs out. He'd given up. He was crying. He was going to run.

He wasn't. Of course he wasn't. If he did he was finished. He was coming round, she realized. Coming round to her side to pull her out, and there was no way she'd be able to cling on once he had a hold: not with him standing and her sitting, and with her ankles tied and all. She'd had it.

Aye, but— She saw a straw of hope and clutched at it. Wait. Keep your head down. Wait. There might be one chance. One slim chance, and it'd be the last. She watched him use his hands to push himself out of his seat, and waited.

Eleven minutes to go, and one–nil down. Eleven minutes, and no injury time because there haven't been any injuries. There'd be injuries if I was playing. That number nine for a start. How can they do it – surrender so tamely to their fate? Division Three without a fight. How does that poem go? Do not go gentle. That's what they're doing – going gentle, the gits. Ten and a half minutes. Two goals. No chance.

Listen to that Bury lot and all, laughing and jeering. Staying up. Not only up but rubbing it in as well.

How can it happen? What's up with the Ointment? Why've they gone quiet? Why don't they storm the barriers and shut the buggers up? Give 'em summat to remember Barfax by? Smash 'em?

Ten minutes. Come on, Town. Oh for God's sake please – come on!

Wait. Wait.

Royston pushed himself forward and up.
His weight was over his feet now and he was
moving round the door, resting his left hand
on top of it. One chance. One go, and if she
fumbled it she was dead.

He took his hand away, moving round the
front of the car. Now! She dived across,
grabbed the handle and slammed the door.

Royston whirled with a cry and lunged for
the handle. Sobbing, Debbie snapped the lock
then turned, flinging herself across the car as
he realized his mistake and ran round the
front. For one dreadful second her fingers
scrabbled as she sought the tiny lever.
Royston came round the bonnet, snarling.
Their eyes met and Debbie saw the flame of
insanity in his. Then she found the catch and
slid it home.

Royston bent, screaming at her through the
glass and pounding it with his fists. 'Open it!
Open the door or I'll smash the window in.'

He would. Of course he would. Debbie slid
across the seat over the gap where the gear-
lever was. She hadn't beaten him. She knew
that. She'd gained a few seconds, that was all.
A few seconds in which to think of something
else.

She glanced through the window. Royston

was casting about him for something to smash it with. Once he smashed it he'd shove his arm in and open the lock and that would be it. Sobbing, she plucked and tore at the wire he'd hobbled her with. As she worked she kept looking out. The wire loosened. As she tore it away Royston straightened, grinning. He'd found a brick.

Desperately she glanced around the inside of the car, seeking a weapon. Her stomach ached, and she hurt dreadfully every time she moved. She fought the urge to throw up, knowing she'd be defenceless if she did.

A shadow fell across her. She looked up. Royston approached the window with the brick in his hand. As she watched, he swung his arm back and then forward. There was a sharp crack and the window exploded inwards showering her with bits of glass. She screamed, and went on screaming as he thrust his arm through the jagged hole he'd made.

25

Seven minutes to go. Bury, in possession, were taking no chances. They began passing the ball back across their own half, taking their time, with the obvious intention of giving it to their goalie. It was a good tactic in the circumstances, but it proved to be their undoing.

They had taken off an injured man and brought on their substitute. This man received the ball and was killing time with it just outside his penalty area when Harris charged him. Whether the man lacked bottle or simply misjudged his back-pass was unclear, but he drove the ball so hard towards his own goal that it skidded between the keeper's legs and on into the net.

The Barfax crowd roared as the referee trotted towards the centre. Brian leapt and cheered, then looked at his watch again. 'Six minutes,' he whispered to himself, clenching his fists and shaking them in front of his face. 'Come on, Town.' He looked up to repeat the three words in the form of a shout, and his words exploded in a blinding flash as a lump of concrete smashed into the side of his head.

'Brian!' Colin cried out in horror as his friend toppled sideways and sprawled motionless on the step. Galvanized by Bury's own goal, Barfax were pressing forward and the fans, on tiptoe and shrieking, noticed nothing. Colin went down on one knee and lifted Brian's head. It rolled limply. Blood oozed from a horrible depression in the left temple. He turned and shouted, but his voice was drowned by another roar as the fans went up for the goal.

26

Debbie slid over into the driver's seat. As she did so, her foot struck something on the floor. The jack-handle. She ducked down and grabbed it. Royston's hand was creeping like a pale spider along the inside of the door, feeling for the catch. She leaned over, raised the weapon and brought it down. Royston screamed with pain and snatched his hand away. A roar came from the direction of the football ground, and for the first time in her life Debbie wished she was there. She had a fleeting picture of Brian in his cap and scarf, standing beside her, and then the window burst on the driver's side and Royston had her by the hair.

She screamed and wriggled and pressed the horn but it was no use. The grip on her hair was relentless. Snarling and cursing, the mad youth wrenched open the door and dragged her kicking into the roadway. She was still holding the jack-handle, but Royston dumped her in the dirt and stamped her hand till she let go. Then he hauled her on to her feet, twisted her arm up her back and began shoving her towards one of the derelict houses. Debbie looked desperately about her in the hope that the noise she'd made had attracted somebody's attention, but the street was empty. Somewhere, a siren wailed. Police perhaps, or an ambulance. But too far away. Too far away.

Royston laughed, briefly because he was winded. 'There's nobody here, kid: just you and me. Soon, there'll be just me. You should've listened to my dad. He told you to stay away from me. I heard him.'

She hung back, digging her heels into the cracks between the setts. Step in a crack, break your mother's back. That's what she'd chanted long ago when the only horrors she knew about were imaginary. Royston jerked her arm and ran her forward, so that she almost tripped over the kerb. A doorless entrance yawned in front of her. Cracked plastic numbers screwed to the doorpost. Twenty-three. He wrenched her arm again, half-lifting her onto the doorstep. As he did so there was a shout from somewhere on the right, and the sound of running feet. He muttered something unintelligible and tried to shove her inside, but she grabbed a doorpost with her free hand and started screaming.

The footsteps grew louder. Royston, sobbing and cursing, struck Debbie's arm again and again with his fist, his eyes staring in the direction of the sounds. Sixty metres away there was a corner. From round this corner a knot of youths appeared, running hard. They swung right and came pounding towards the pair on the step. They wore the scarves and caps of Bury AFC, and hard on their heels came a second group, whooping and shouting, their Barfax colours streaming in the wind.

As the first group approached, Royston gave up his hold on Debbie and turned, running towards the car. Debbie, sick and dizzy, slumped against the doorpost crying, 'Help – help me, please!'

The youths, hard-pressed and in danger, were not inclined to stop. If her presence registered at all, it was as some kid playing silly games. They began running past, breathing hard.

Debbie flapped a hand towards the car. 'Stop him!' she cried. 'Stop the killer.' Royston was inside the car and she heard the engine cough as he twisted the key in the ignition. Something in her tone or appearance must have told the youths this was no game, because they clattered to a stop and stood, gaping first at her and then at the car as their pursuers arrived on the scene.

Barry Weatherall couldn't understand it. One minute he'd got this Third Division rubbish on the run, and the next here they were, loitering on the pavement, waiting to be smashed to pulp. And he'd seen this scruffy-looking kid somewhere before and all. He glared at her.

'What's up?'

Debbie pointed to the car. 'Him – he killed

Leanne Stanton and that other girl. He was going to kill me.'

Weatherall scowled. 'Are you having me on or summat?'

'No!' She was crying. 'Look at me.' She spread her arms and looked down at herself. Weatherall looked. Her skirt was torn, she was wet, and there were cuts and scratches and red blotches all over her arms and legs.

'Bloody hell!' He turned. Royston had got the car started and was doing a u-turn, skidding and bucking through the debris. In a single motion, Weatherall snatched up a broken roof-slate and shied it at the windscreen, which shattered. With a screech of brakes the car mounted the pavement, rammed a disued junction-box and stalled.

'Come on!' Weatherall pelted towards the vehicle and the others followed. The driver's door opened and Royston fell out. He sat for a moment in the dirt, staring at the approaching youths. Then he scrambled to his feet, dived back into the car and slammed the door.

The rival fans surrounded the car. 'OK,' said Weatherall. 'He'll do in there for now. Keep an eye on him while I see to this kid. You.' He nodded towards a Bury supporter. 'Run back to Hillside and fetch the coppers. Tell 'em we've got the feller that's been doing lasses in. Oh, and tell 'em there's an injured lass here, and all.'

He walked over and looked down at Debbie. She was sitting doubled up on the doorstep with her head on her arms, weeping.

'It's OK,' he grunted. 'We've got him. He can't hurt you any more. Here.' He took off his jacket and bent, intending to drape it round her shoulders.

'No!' She recoiled from him, shuddering. 'Don't touch me. I'm all right. Just don't touch me, OK?'

27

They put her in the back of a panda-car and took her up to St Luke's. She was wrapped in a police raincoat and a policewoman sat beside her. She didn't feel like talking, but the policewoman was gentle and it turned out she'd once been a pupil at Debbie's school.

'We will have to ask you a lot of questions eventually,' she said. 'But we're going to let a doctor have a look at you first. We've sent a car for your mum and dad, and I expect they'll be waiting for you at the hospital.'

They were. As she walked into Casualty, holding on to the policewoman's arm, they came and hugged her and started fussing – asking question after question without waiting for her to answer. Mum was crying, and Dad kept going on about what he'd do to Royston Ambler if he got his hands on him. In the end, the policewoman had to make them sit down. 'Give her time,' she said. 'She's been through a nasty experience.'

She sat on a long seat. The policewoman sat beside her and Mum and Dad sat opposite, gazing at her through worried eyes. She felt detached, as though none of this was really happening. The grey linoleum on the floor was very shiny. She wondered if Brian's mum polished it when she worked here in the evenings.

A nurse came and took her into a little room with bright lights and a high, narrow bed. She had to take her clothes off and lie on the bed. The nurse helped her, as though she was three years old. There was blood on some of her things.

A doctor came and examined her, asking her questions in a quiet voice as she worked. Some of the things she did hurt. Then the nurse came back and bathed her cuts and dabbed on some stinging stuff and dressed them. She had an injection. And all the time, it was like it was happening to somebody else and Debbie was only watching.

The nurse covered her with a red blanket and left her. She could hear the doctor talking to her parents outside, though she couldn't make out what was being said. She didn't know what she was supposed to do. The lights were too bright for sleeping, and anyway she couldn't have slept. She couldn't stop shivering. She kept going over and over what had happened, like an action-replay. Now and then, great shudders ran through her and she found herself crying.

After a while she heard loud voices. It sounded as though the waiting-room was full of boys, shouting and clomping about on the glossy linoleum. Am I dreaming? she wondered. Or am I going mad? 'He's our mate,' she heard one of them say. Somebody hushed him, and she heard the doctor's voice, gentle but firm, saying, 'I'm sorry, but you're too late. He was transferred to Pinderfields in an extremely critical condition and I think I should warn you that he'll very likely die.'

A girl's voice, shrill and querulous. 'Brian? He can't die. I was talking to him an hour ago. He can't die.'

Debbie lay rigid. Brian. The girl had said Brian. She strained her ears to hear more but the doctor had managed to quieten the visitors and was speaking softly herself. She shook her head. It isn't him. Why should it be? There's loads of Brians. But even as she reasoned with herself she was sitting up, gathering the blanket round her. Sliding off the bed.

Her arm was stiffening up, she hurt in a hundred places and the lino was cold under her feet. 'It's not him,' she whispered, crossing the room, 'you're acting daft.'

She eased down the handle and opened the door a crack. Colin was standing two metres away, tears on his cheeks. 'No,' she whispered, shaking her head. 'Oh no.' She flung the door open. Jeannette was there, and Lee, and Jonathan. They turned towards her. The doctor turned too, surprise and concern on her face. Her parents jumped up from the bench they'd been sitting on and her father hurried forward, reaching for her with his arms.

'No.' She retreated, shaking her head. 'No, no, no.' It wasn't real. She'd opened the door and stepped out into a dream. A nightmare. The thing to do was to shut it again. Shut it out. She slammed the door and pressed her back against it, hooking the fingers of both hands behind her bottom teeth. The red blanket slipped from her shoulders. Great, choking sobs convulsed her and she slid very slowly down the door and sat down on the crumpled blanket.

PART FOUR

STAYING UP

1

It was an autumn evening, and Debbie was in Ferncliffe Cemetery. It was dusk already. There were fallen leaves in the grass and mist across the valley, but it was still hard for Debbie to believe it was October. Time didn't exist in Wynfield Mount, and she'd lost a whole summer. They'd drugged her up to the eyeballs and put her in Group Therapy and left her to wander in the grounds, which were like the gardens of some stately home, and then last week they'd discharged her, cured. Of what, she wasn't sure. Mum called it 'Your illness', but she hadn't felt ill. She'd just gone on feeling like she felt after the lads rescued her from Royston Ambler: detached, uninvolved, as though it was a film she was watching which would end soon and she'd walk out into the real world again. It had stayed like that till the day Mum and Dad came and told her Brian was going to be all right. After that she'd started making progress and now here she was standing in Ferncliffe Cemetery at dusk, talking to a dead girl. It seemed a pretty crazy thing to be doing if you thought about it, so maybe she wasn't cured at all. On the other hand, she couldn't have come here six months ago or even three. Not at dusk. Not anytime, to the place where Leanne was, and Janet Stobbs whom she'd never known. The place she'd be lying in herself if that game had gone into injury time. She couldn't have come here three months ago yet here she was, and maybe that proved she was getting better. Anyway . . .

She laid the half-bunch of dahlias on the mound. She'd meant the whole bunch for Leanne, but then she'd remembered Janet Stobbs and split it: half for Leanne, half for Janet. It was only fair.

'Hi, Deb.'

She spun round and there was Brian, standing in the long brown grass, looking at her.

'Hello, Brian. How's it going?' Her heart was racing from the suddenness of his voice. It did that when anything startled her. She had tablets for it.

'Fine. You?' His face was thin and very white, and he was wearing what looked like a cyclist's headguard.

She nodded. 'I'm OK. Do you think it's crazy to talk to somebody who's dead?'

He smiled, shaking his head. 'No. If I was dead and you came to talk to me, I'd be glad.'

'I'm glad you're not. Dead, I mean. I thought you were, you know.'

188

'Yes. It was touch and go for a bit, down Pinderfields. Hey listen.'

'What?'

'I called round your place. I was scared. I thought your folks'd tell me to piss off but they were really nice. Asked me all about my head, and if I was feeling OK now, and would I be going back to school. Then they told me where to find you, like they'd always been mad keen on me.'

Debbie nodded. 'They're on football fans. Off polite young men with cars, and on football fans. I don't need to tell you why.'

'No, you don't. And what about you; are you on football fans?'

She dropped her eyes. After a moment she said, 'I'm off lads, Brian. I don't feel right when there's one near me. I don't feel right now.'

He looked at her. 'You mean you think I – you mean you're nervous, just because I'm here?'

She nodded. 'More than nervous. More like . . .' She shrugged. 'I can't explain. I don't feel right, that's all.'

'Yeah. Well, I mean it's understandable. Only I was hoping – y'know – you and me.' He smiled wryly. 'I wouldn't be mad on football, Deb – not like before.'

'Oh, Brian.' She shook her head. 'It's not that. That doesn't matter to me now.'

'You've changed, then.'

She nodded. 'All that time in Wynfield Mount, when I thought I'd never see you again, I kept remembering the last thing I said to you. D'you remember?'

He looked down, biting his lip. 'No. No I don't, Deb. I can't remember a lot of the stuff from just before the – accident. They say it'll come back gradually. What did you say?'

'I said I hoped they'd lose ten–nil. I didn't mean it. I was mad, that's all. Only all that time, I thought I'd never get the chance to tell you. Anyway, they stayed up, Brian, and I'm glad, and if you and me – if you and me ever do go out again and you want to go to football, I won't mind. Only, it might be a long time, Brian.'

He nodded. 'I know, and I'll be around, however long it is.' He grinned. 'I'm glad they stayed up too, but not as glad as I would've been if none of this had happened to us. It doesn't seem all that important any more. Like, if one of us had died, it'd have been for something that didn't really matter. Not really. Know what I mean?'

She nodded. 'I think so, yes. Staying up's important; it's the most important thing there is, only you've got to stay up yourself. It's no use latching on to a football team or something and thinking they can do it for you, because that's just a sort of illusion. Hey.'

She grinned, blushing. 'Listen to me. I'm getting to sound like old Dodgson.'

Brian smiled. 'Yeah. You're right, though. It's a game. Just a game. What matters is us staying up – you and me. Right?'

'Right.'

He reached for her hand but she withdrew it and they walked along the path together without touching.

'We could try for the Premier Division,' she said.

'Aye.' He grinned. 'Or make 'em print the league table t'other way up.'

When they got to the gate the man was there, waiting to lock up. He nodded, and gave them a curt 'G'night'.

They walked down to the bus stop and stood looking into the valley. It had filled up with mist, so that a stranger standing here would not know there was anything down there at all, except that ropes of amber light showed how roads came swooping out of the surrounding hills, converging on the town.

Like cables, mused Debbie. A web of cables, mooring the town to the hills. And if you screw your eyes up and look carefully you can see a spire or a chimney or a pylon; a bit of Barfax piercing the mist, to show the lines still hold.

THE END

IF YOU ENJOYED READING THIS BOOK, WHY NOT TRY READING ANOTHER TITLE FROM CORGI BOOKS?

0552 528390	A.N.T.I.D.O.T.E.	Malorie Blackman	£3.99
0552 527513	HACKER	Malorie Blackman	£3.99
0552 527971	A BONE FROM A DRY SEA	Peter Dickinson	£3.99
0552 52719X	A.K.	Peter Dickinson	£2.99
0552 526096	EVA	Peter Dickinson	£3.99
0552 528447	SHADOW OF A HERO	Peter Dickinson	£3.99
0552 545015	GODHANGER	Dick King-Smith	£3.99
0552 527521	THE CARPET PEOPLE	Terry Pratchett	£3.99
0552 139262	ONLY YOU CAN SAVE MANKIND	Terry Pratchett	£3.99
0552 52968	JOHNNY AND THE BOMB	Terry Pratchett	£3.99
0552 527408	JOHNNY AND THE DEAD	Terry Pratchett	£3.99